Missy Piggle-Wiggle

and the

Sticky-Fingers Cure

ANN M. MARTIN

with ANNIE PARNELL

illustrated by BEN HATKE

Feiwel and Friends
New York

This book is for my Soul Sisters:
Liz, Jean, and Emma, with love
—A. M. M.

For my husband. Your patience, love, and
support make even the most upside-down days
feel right-side-up.
—A. P.

Based on the Mrs. Piggle-Wiggle series of
books and characters created by Betty MacDonald
and Anne MacDonald Canham

A FEIWEL AND FRIENDS BOOK

An imprint of Macmillan Publishing Group, LLC

MISSY PIGGLE-WIGGLE AND THE STICKY-FINGERS CURE. Text copyright © 2018 by Ann M. Martin, Inc. and Elliam Corp. Illustrations copyright © 2018 by Ben Hatke. All rights reserved. Rights in the original characters created by Betty MacDonald and Anne MacDonald Canham are reserved to the creators. Printed in the United States of America by LSC Communications, Harrisonburg, Virginia. For information, address Feiwel and Friends, 175 Fifth Avenue, New York, N.Y. 10010.

Our books may be purchased in bulk for promotional, educational, or business use. Please contact your local bookseller or the Macmillan Corporate and Premium Sales Department at (800) 221-7945 ext. 5442 or by e-mail at MacmillanSpecialMarkets@macmillan.com.

Library of Congress Cataloging-in-Publication Data

Names: Martin, Ann M., 1955- author. | Parnell, Annie, author. | Hatke, Ben, illustrator.
Title: Missy Piggle-Wiggle and the Sticky-Fingers Cure / Ann M. Martin ; with Annie Parnell ; Illustrations by Ben Hatke.
Description: First edition. | New York : Feiwel and Friends, 2018. | Summary: Even though she, her upside-down house, and its animal occupants are under quarantine with the Winter Effluvia, Missy Piggle-Wiggle manages to dispense cures to the misbehaving children of Little Spring Valley.
Identifiers: LCCN 2018002550 | ISBN 978-1-250-13229-1 (hardcover) | ISBN 978-1-250-13230-7 (ebook)
Subjects: | CYAC: Behavior—Fiction. | Magic—Fiction. | Humorous stories.
Classification: LCC PZ7.M3567585 Mk 2018 | DDC [Fic]—dc23
LC record available at https://lccn.loc.gov/2018002550

Book design by Eileen Savage

Feiwel and Friends logo designed by Filomena Tuosto

First edition, 2018

10 9 8 7 6 5 4 3 2 1

CONTENTS

CONTENTS

Dear Missy,

You'll never guess where I'm writing from. The deck of a ship. And in case you're wondering, no, it isn't a pirate ship, although in the distance I can see the back end of a pirate ship—the very same ship from which your great-uncle, my beloved husband, Mr. Piggle-Wiggle, was recently rescued. The ship is now retreating with its flags flying low.

As you know, in matters concerning pirates, I must be discreet, so I can't tell you how the rescue took place or even what sea we are now sailing. The important thing is that Mr. Piggle-Wiggle is safe and we are together again.

I hope you'll understand what I'm about to say next. Mr. Piggle-Wiggle and I would dearly like to spend some time in each other's company, sailing the world. Imagine the places we can explore! Imagine the animals; imagine the desert and the mountains and the tropics. Will you be able to carry on at the upside-down house? I promise to write and tell you of our adventures.

Your loving and grateful Auntie

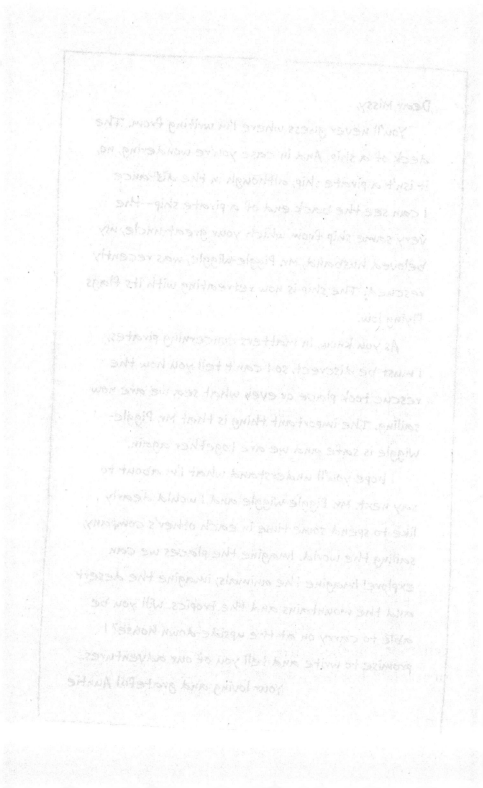

1

The Winter Effluvia

MOST PEOPLE WOULD be surprised if they dropped a piece of bread in the toaster and a minute later out popped not toast, but a letter. Missy Piggle-Wiggle wasn't surprised, though. That was because she lived in an upside-down house with a talking parrot and a pig who could read and liked to drink coffee. And anyway, Missy was a little bit magic.

The day had started off unremarkably, at least as unremarkably as any day in an upside-down house. Missy had woken to the sound of *hee-haw, hee-haw.* The sound came not from the barn outside, where there were plenty of animals, but from the very walls of the house. The house had a mind of its own, and on this morning it had decided that Missy should get up with a *hee-haw* at 6:39.

Hee-haw, hee-haw!

Missy rolled over in her warm bed. "Thank you, House," she said, even though she had thought she might sleep until 7:04.

Lightfoot the cat, who had been curled up on Missy's head, tumbled off. She let out an annoyed *mrrow* and jumped to the floor, where she sat flicking her tail and licking her paws. At the foot of the bed, Wag yawned and stretched and gave a little woof. Missy leaned down to scratch between his ears.

Hee-haw, hee-haw!

"House, for heaven's sake, I'm awake!"

"A ridiculous poem!" squawked Penelope the parrot, flying into the bedroom. "For heaven's sake, I'm awake! For heaven's sake, I'm awake!"

"Good morning to you, too, Penelope." Missy pulled aside the curtains. "It's still dark outside," she grumbled to the house.

A gentle knock came at the door, and in stepped

Lester the pig, looking glum. Often he brought Missy coffee, but this morning he stood droopily by her bed.

"Didn't you sleep?" Missy asked him. She gave him a pat.

Lester shrugged his hairy shoulders.

"Almost breakfast time," said Missy brightly.

The animals left the room, stepping over the doorway. That was the thing about an upside-down house: Nothing was exactly where people from right-side-up houses expected it to be. There was a step in each doorway since the top of the door was at the bottom and the bottom was at the top. The floors were the ceilings, and the ceilings were the floors. The windows were either too high or too low. Light fixtures grew out of the floor, and the doorknobs were hard to reach, especially if you were a pig. The chimney burrowed into the ground and so did the roof, while the bottom of the house stood proudly in the sky.

This was exactly the sort of house Missy's great-aunt, Mrs. Piggle-Wiggle, had dreamed of when she was a little girl, and so when she married Mr. Piggle-Wiggle, he had built it for her. It was the only upside-down house in Little Spring Valley and maybe in all the world, although it was hard to know that for certain.

Missy opened her closet, stooped down, and tugged at the string attached to the light bulb on the floor. The bulb lit up her dresses from below. "Hmm," she said, and chose her warmest winter dress—the knitted one with silver spangles at the bottom—and her sensible pink boots. Then she made her bed and straightened her dresser. Before she left the room, she stopped to examine her cabinet of cures. The cabinet was wooden and painted a pleasant shade of blue. And it was locked. The cures inside were magic and didn't belong in anyone's hands except Missy's. Missy removed the small brass key she wore around her neck, inserted the key in the lock, opened the cabinet doors, and surveyed the contents.

"I wonder," Missy murmured. "I wonder who will need curing next."

There were many strange and wonderful things about Little Spring Valley, and one of them was that Missy Piggle-Wiggle—like her great-aunt before her—was renowned for her ability to cure children of such afflictions as spying and whining, of gum smacking and smarty-pantsiness. Missy had a cure for just about everything, and the parents of the children needing cures were always pleased and surprised to find that when their children no longer spied or whined or smacked their gum or bored people with endless lectures about the tomato and whether it was a fruit or a vegetable, they loved Missy even more than before. She was very popular with the children in town.

Missy looked at the rows of potions in the cupboard, the bottles of pills, the little vials of pink and blue and purple liquids, each with a label carefully lettered by Missy: TARDINESS, BRAGGING, MESSINESS, CHORE FORGETTING. Sometimes one of the bottles would work itself to the front of a shelf as a sign of what cure might be needed next, but this morning everything was in order. "Hmm. I wonder," Missy said again.

Missy walked along the hallway to the staircase, pleased to see that the carpet was raised just half an inch above the floor. Sometimes the house floated the carpets or the furniture all the way up to the ceiling, but not today. Today the house was in order, too.

Missy walked quickly down the staircase, which was an upstairs staircase when she went down and a downstairs staircase when she went up. She hurried into the kitchen, where Lightfoot, Wag, and Penelope were waiting for breakfast. Lester was standing over the funny old black stove, stirring a pot of oatmeal.

"Thank you, Lester," said Missy, and prepared dishes of cat food, dog food, and parrot food. Then she sat at the table and dropped a slice of bread in the toaster, and a minute later the letter popped out. Missy reached for it. "Oh, good. Here's Auntie's letter at last. I wondered where it had gotten to." Weeks earlier, Missy had received an empty envelope in the mail, an envelope addressed in her great-aunt's handwriting. Now here, popping out of the toaster, was the missing letter.

Lester pointed at the letter with a front hoof, so Missy read it aloud to him. "It seems I'm to be here for the long haul," she told him when she had finished. "Imagine, sailing around the world. I hope Auntie sends us souvenirs from time to time."

Lester turned back to the stove and continued stirring the oatmeal. "Lester?" said Missy. "Isn't this exciting news?"

Lester offered her a small smile over his shoulder.

"Are you all—" Missy started to ask him, but she

was interrupted by Penelope, who had finished her breakfast and was whooshing through the kitchen screeching, "I need a tissue!"

"A tissue? Whatever for?" asked Missy. She had never once seen Penelope blow her beak. Missy thought that Lester and Penelope were not quite themselves that morning. She looked out the window at a gray and dreary day. Perhaps it was the weather.

Missy turned her mind to other matters. She wrote a note to herself to remember to ask Melody Flowers if she had enjoyed her sleepover at Tulip Goodenough's house. Melody was new to town and still having just the teensiest bit of trouble making new friends. Missy spent the rest of the morning taking care of the animals in the barn and baking gingerbread for the children who would stop by the upside-down house after school. Children always stopped by her house. This was because Missy wasn't like any other adult they knew. She kept a box of clothes for dressing up, invented wonderful games such as Pirate Ball and Sliding Down the Stairs, and encouraged the climbing of trees and shouting and getting dirty. And she was always available for a chat if someone was having a hard time. The nice thing about Missy Piggle-Wiggle was that, unlike some adults, she took children and their troubles very seriously.

After lunch, which Missy and Lester ate together in the kitchen, Missy clipped Wag's leash to his collar. "I'm going into town!" she called. Then she frowned at Lester. "You didn't eat much."

Lester shrugged again. Then he waved a hoof at her.

"Bye!" squawked Penelope.

"House?" said Missy. "Did you hear me?"

Ordinarily the house replied with the flick of a window shade or the rattling of a floorboard, but today there was nothing.

"All right," said Missy anyway. "I'll see you later."

Wag bounded out the door, across the porch, and down the steps to the yard. Then he bounded along the path to the sidewalk and turned left, going so fast that Missy had to run to keep up with him. They hurried past the houses of Little Spring Valley, and Missy thought the town looked rather desolate, even when she passed Melody's house, which was painted pink and yellow and blue. It was that time in early winter when all the trees and plants had turned brown and tan and gray, and no snow had fallen to brighten things up. The wind blew old dead leaves every which way, and the sky seemed to have lowered so that you could almost touch the damp clouds. Missy felt hemmed in.

Wag was a smart dog, and when he came to Juniper Street, he turned right all by himself. They had reached the main street, with its shops and businesses and restaurants, the library and the post office, and at one end A to Z Books, which was where Missy and Wag were headed.

Wag walked more slowly now. He and Missy scuffed through the fallen leaves, and Missy noticed that in the windows of several stores the Halloween decorations had been replaced with turkeys and Santas and menorahs and twinkling lights.

"The lights are cheerful, aren't they, Wag?" she said.

Missy waved to Aunt Martha in Aunt Martha's General Store as they passed by. She called hello to Dean and Jean Bean, the owners of Bean's Coffee Shop. At last she reached the bookstore. She opened the door, which sneezed loudly to alert Harold Spectacle that a customer had arrived.

"Missy!" called Harold from behind the counter. "What a nice surprise on a chilly, gray day."

"Wag and I are here for a quick visit before school lets out."

"Is anything on your mind?"

"As a matter of fact, yes." Missy removed her winter coat, which she liked because it was striped with colors that reminded her of an erupting volcano. She sat down behind the counter on a stool next to Harold. "Something is wrong, but I'm not sure what."

"Then how do you know something is wrong?"

"Because everything seems . . . off."

Harold regarded Missy. On this afternoon he was wearing his usual top hat, but his vest was a brilliant yellow, and in each buttonhole was a large purple flower.

"Maybe it's the weather," Harold replied. "It's so gray. That's why I'm wearing one of my spring outfits."

Missy thought Harold looked like a crocus but didn't say so. "No," she said after a moment. "It isn't the weather. Or anyway, it isn't *just* the weather. Lester isn't eating much today, and he didn't fix himself any coffee. House seems awfully quiet, except for waking me up like a braying donkey early this morning. And Penelope has been flying around saying she needs a tissue."

"For her beak?"

"I suppose so. On the other hand, yesterday she complained that she felt tired and run-down, and I started to worry, but then she said, 'Feeling low? Don't despair. Chewable Vitabitties are just the ticket for beating the blahs.'"

"Ah. The Vitabitties commercial," said Harold. "Still . . ." He looked thoughtful. "Are you quite sure it isn't the Winter Effluvia? That could explain everything."

"The Winter Effluvia," Missy repeated. "I heard Auntie mention that once, I think, but I've never had it myself."

"This is exactly the time of year when it strikes, although luckily it doesn't strike very often. Perhaps once in a generation."

"I seem to recall that the Effluvia is rather contagious." Missy reached for Harold's hand.

"Unfortunately, yes. And there's no cure for it. One must simply live with the symptoms until they go away on their own."

"And what are the symptoms?"

"That's the strange thing. The Effluvia affects everyone differently."

An uncomfortable thought squirmed into Missy's head. "I think Auntie told me about a friend of hers who caught the Effluvia and became a back-talker. All day long for two weeks, he back-talked to everyone. His wife would say, 'Dear, did you remember to drop off the dry cleaning?' and he would reply, 'What do I look like? A taxi?' He sassed and back-talked and back-talked and sassed for fourteen days, and on the fifteenth day, he woke up and he was himself again."

"I had the Effluvia when I was a child," said Harold, "and all I had was a bad cold."

"Did your family catch the Effluvia from you?"

"Yes. My brother temporarily lost the ability to tell the truth, and my sister could only bark."

"And there's no cure?"

"No cure. But don't worry. As I said, the Effluvia doesn't strike often," said Harold, patting Missy's hand. "Maybe you're worrying for nothing."

"I hope so." Missy glanced at the clock. "Goodness! School will be out in just a few minutes. I'd better get back to the house."

"If you see Melody, tell her the book she ordered came in."

"I will," replied Missy, and rushed home, scolding herself along the way. "Don't be such a worrywart," she said aloud. So what if Penelope was quoting vitamin commercials and the house had been braying like a donkey? There was no sense worrying about every little thing. This wasn't the Winter Effluvia; it was simply life in the upside-down house. "You'll work yourself into a lather," Missy added as she turned onto her street.

~~~~~

By the time Missy and Wag were hurrying along the path to the upside-down house, Missy could hear happy shouts as the children of Little Spring Valley ran home from school. She let herself inside without so much as a creak or a groan from the house and called to Lester, who she found dozing in an armchair. He waved to her but went back to sleep.

A moment later there was the sound of footsteps on the porch, and Penelope flew past Missy squawking, "Veronica Cupcake is here!" Before Missy had time to thank her, Penelope added, "Melody Flowers is here!" Two seconds later she added, "And here are Rusty Goodenough and Egmont Dolittle!"

Missy opened the door, and in rushed the children.

"Is there gingerbread?" asked Veronica.

"Can we read together?" asked Melody.

"Could I take Wag for a walk?" asked Rusty.

"Can we make a trampoline with your couch cushions?" asked Egmont.

"Yes, yes, yes, and yes," replied Missy.

Suddenly the house seemed lighter and Missy felt brighter. She served the gingerbread, and Veronica, who was prone to tantrums, cleared the table afterward without a whisper of complaint. Missy began reading *Lassie* to Melody and the three Freeforall children, who had shown up during the gingerbread. The trampoliners jumped and jumped on the cushions, and when Egmont accidentally crash-landed in Missy's lap, none of the other children laughed at him (although Missy heard faint gleeful cackling from Penelope as she flew out of the room).

The afternoon seemed like any other, and Missy

relaxed—until dinnertime came and the children began to leave, and the house let them go without a sound while Lester continued to lie mournfully on the couch.

Missy looked around the quiet house. "Who's ready for supper?" she asked the animals.

"Feeling tired? Feeling blue?" screeched Penelope from the back of a chair. "Chewable Vitabitties are just for you!"

"I wonder," said Missy again. "I wonder."

2

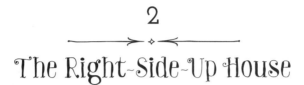

The Right-Side-Up House

TWO DAYS LATER Missy Piggle-Wiggle awoke on a pleasant Friday morning, reached for her watch, and discovered that it was nearly 7:30. "House!" she cried. "You let me oversleep!" She listened for some sort of reply from the house but heard nothing. She leaped out of bed and stepped over the chandelier on the floor, then tripped because the chandelier was missing.

"This must be a dream," Missy murmured. She stared down at the floor. "How on earth could a chandelier disappear?"

Wag, snoozing in his spot at the end of the bed, lifted his head and wrinkled his eyebrows.

Missy pulled open the curtains and discovered that her window was a foot higher off the floor than usual. Outside, though, the sun was shining and the yard looked as bare and wintry as ever. She glimpsed Warren and Evelyn Goose and Martha and Millard Mallard searching for corn in the barnyard. They seemed perfectly fine.

"Aha!" Missy said to Wag. "This is the work of House. House must be feeling better and is playing tricks again." But Missy's tingling fingertips told her that was not right. She hurried to her closet to get dressed, felt around on the floor for the string attached to the bulb, and couldn't find it. She couldn't find the bulb either. She shone a flashlight on the floor and saw nothing but shoes. Dressed in her nightgown and an old flannel robe, she stepped through the doorway into the hall—and gasped because there was nothing to step over.

Penelope came swooping along the hallway then. "Look up! Look up!" she squawked.

Missy tipped her head back. That was when she saw that the door was no longer upside down. She went back into her room and looked at the ceiling. There was the chandelier. She stepped into her closet, and the string attached to the light bulb swatted her in the face. The bulb was high above her head.

"My stars and garters," she said. Then she added, "I never."

The upside-down house had become a right-side-up house. The ceilings were the ceilings and the floors were the floors.

Missy ran down the stairs, which this morning felt like downstairs stairs and not upstairs stairs. In the parlor, she tripped once more, this time in the spot where another chandelier should have sprouted but was missing. She opened the front door and ran across the porch and partway down the path, not caring that her bare feet were pounding along freezing stones, and also not caring that people on their way to work could see her wearing her fuzzy yellow bathrobe that made her look like one of the ducklings the Mallards hatched each spring. She stopped, turned, and stared at the upside-down house. Its chimney pointed to the sky. So did its roof. Not a single thing about it was upside down.

Missy walked slowly back inside and closed the

door gently behind her. "House? Are you angry?" she asked as she made her way into the parlor. She grabbed the back of the couch and held on tight since she felt somewhat dizzy from all the right-side-up-ness. "House?" she asked again. She waited for a reply from the house, for a lamp to switch itself on or for the tea-kettle to whistle in the kitchen. "Please tell me this is a trick," said Missy eventually, even though her finger-tips told her that it was not.

As soon as Missy had fed the animals, she sat down at the table in the kitchen with a cup of coffee and her phone. Lester sat opposite her. He was slowly stirring coffee of his own. He stirred and stirred and stirred. The cup was full.

"Aren't you going to drink that?" Missy asked.

Lester took the cup delicately between his front hooves and raised it to his lips. He took an ant-sized sip and set the cup back on the table.

Missy sighed. Then, even though it was still quite early, she picked up her phone and called Harold Spec-tacle.

"Missy?" said Harold instantly. "Is something wrong?"

Missy hesitated. "I know you're just about to open the store, but, yes, I believe something is wrong."

"Are you at home? Shall I come over?"

"Yes, please."

Missy took her coffee into the parlor. She clutched at the backs of chairs and couches in order to keep from falling. "I feel like I'm on board a ship," she remarked to Wag.

Wag glanced at her, then made a wide arc around the empty spot where the chandelier should have been.

"Silly boy," said Missy. "Nothing is there."

She stood at the window with her coffee, looking out at the street. Presently she caught sight of Harold. He was hurrying along in his top hat and his winter tuxedo, the wool one he had had specially made for cold weather. He was in such a hurry that, Missy realized, he had forgotten to bring his cane, which didn't matter one bit, since he didn't actually need it.

Missy opened the front door, then watched in surprise as Harold rushed right by the house.

"Harold?" Missy called. "Harold!"

Harold stopped and looked about in surprise. "Missy?"

"Back here!"

Harold turned around. He stood stock-still. After a long moment, he said, "Oh, my," as he gazed at the house.

"I know," said Missy miserably from the porch.

Harold ran along the front path. He was used to the stones wavering and wobbling beneath his feet, but they remained in place, which caused Harold to trip four times before he reached the porch. "First day with my new feet," he murmured, blushing. Then he looked above his head. He glanced to his left at the chimney. He looked at Missy. He opened and closed his mouth several times. At last he said, "It's right side up."

Missy nodded.

"Inside, too?"

"Yes."

Missy ushered Harold in, and he gazed at the ceilings and the floors and the windows. "Oh, my," he said again.

"What do you think has happened?" Missy asked.

"I don't know. I've lived in Little Spring Valley my entire life, and this has always been an upside-down house."

Missy nodded. "House hasn't given me a sign about what's wrong. Do you think this is . . ." She couldn't bear to finish the sentence.

"The Effluvia?" Harold finished for her.

Missy nodded.

"Could be. How do the animals seem?"

"Something is definitely wrong with Lester."

"How about you?"

"Me? I feel fine."

"Good, good," said Harold, but Missy noticed that he was backing ever so slowly toward the door. As he did so, his hand crept toward the pocket of his pants and withdrew a handkerchief. He pressed it to his nose and mouth. "Lovely to see you," he said, "but I really deed to opedd the store dow."

"What?" asked Missy.

Harold removed the hankie long enough to gasp out, "I need to open the store. Gotta go." He returned the hankie to his face. "Call if you deed adythig. Bye!"

Missy watched him trip along the path. He didn't put the handkerchief back in his pocket until he was safely on the sidewalk. Then he ran as fast as he could.

"This is not good," Missy said to Wag, who was at

her side. She continued to stand in the doorway and noticed that the cars driving down the street slowed when they reached her house, and people opened their windows and gawked. One car stopped entirely, and a woman leaned out and snapped a picture.

Missy sighed and closed the door. "All right," she said to Wag, who appeared to be listening to her. "I need to determine if anyone else in this house has the Effluvia." She patted him. "You seem fine. You ate a good breakfast. And all the outside animals seem fine. Lightfoot seems fine, too, but something is going on with Lester. And Penelope . . . well, who can tell with her?"

Penelope swooped into the parlor then, aiming for a landing on the chandelier. She remembered too late that the chandelier was above her, not below, and she skidded under a table and fell over. She flapped her wings as she got to her feet. "Confound it!"

"Penelope? How are *you* feeling?" Missy asked cautiously.

"All in a muddle," she replied. "All in a muddle."

Missy watched Penelope very closely that morning. She watched her while she ate and while she snoozed and while she jumped up and down on Wag's head until Wag shook himself and she slipped off. "How are you feeling now?" Missy kept asking. Penelope's answer was different every time.

"Under the weather."

"Over the top."

"A bit wobbly."

"Right as rain."

"Fit as a fiddle."

Missy didn't know what to think.

She and Lester ate lunch in the kitchen. Missy thought Lester seemed perkier, although she noticed that his entire lunch consisted of lukewarm liquids—lukewarm soup, lukewarm juice, and lukewarm coffee. She was just deciding that maybe the animals had escaped the Effluvia after all when Lightfoot ambled into the kitchen and suddenly floated to the ceiling.

Missy stared up at her. Sometimes when the house was feeling frisky, it would float a couch with Lester resting on it up to the ceiling, or a bed with Wag sleeping on it. But normally the animals didn't float on their own.

"Lightfoot?" said Missy. "Lightfoot, come down from there!"

Lightfoot looked primly at the kitchen below. She curled her tail around her front legs as if she were sitting on the floor. She licked one front paw. Then she spotted a fly on the ceiling, swatted it, and ate it. A moment later, she yawned, stretched, and began walking along the air. She came to the top of the refrigerator and curled up on it.

"Lightfoot," said Missy, reaching into the refrigerator. "Lightfoot, I have a treat. Would you like a piece of chicken?" She let Lightfoot sniff the chicken, then set it on the floor. "If you want it, you have to come down here."

Lightfoot stood. She leaped off the refrigerator—and landed in the air next to Missy's head so that they were eye to eye. She looked at the chicken below and meowed.

"Uh-oh," said Missy. But she didn't panic. She hurried to her bedroom and inspected the rows of bottles in her cure cabinet. "Ah. Here we are." She removed a small vial labeled ANTI-FLOTATION and rushed it to the kitchen, where she squirted two drops onto the chicken and handed it up to Lightfoot, who was back on the refrigerator. Lightfoot ate it in one gulp.

"Feel any different?" Missy asked.

Lightfoot began to purr and floated upward until her head bumped the ceiling.

Missy set the bottle on the table. "That is a one hundred percent guaranteed remedy, and it isn't working," she said, which was how Missy knew that Lightfoot had caught the Effluvia from the house.

Some decisions are made easily but are difficult to carry out. And some decisions are made with great difficulty but are simple to carry out. Missy's decision to place the house and everyone in it under quarantine was the latter sort. She thought and thought and thought about how she should handle the arrival of the Effluvia. She thought about how contagious it was, how the only cure for it was time, and how she certainly didn't want anyone to catch it from Lightfoot or the house. She thought about the children of Little Spring Valley who stopped by her house every day after school, how they would miss their visits, and how disappointed they would be if they couldn't come inside. She thought about not being able to walk to Juniper Street with Wag and about how she would miss her own visits with Harold Spectacle. She thought about how long the quarantine might last if every resident of the right-side-up upside-down house caught the Effluvia, one after the other.

"The quarantine could go on for weeks, even months," she said sadly to Lester, who was once again lying on the couch. "But I know what I must do."

The next part was easy. Missy found two large pieces of cardboard among the stacks of art supplies she kept on hand for children who wanted to make dollhouses or masks or scenery for puppet shows. Then she found a fat red marker and lettered two signs. The first one read:

> # Quarantine:
> ## No admittance!

The second one read:

Closed
due to Effluvia!

Missy posted one sign on her front door and the other in one of the front windows. The signs had been up for exactly twenty minutes when she heard the first knock. It was accompanied by a very loud voice calling, "Missy? Missy!"

Missy peered through the window in the door. When the door had been upside down, Missy could see only feet through the window. Today she peered at the top of Veronica Cupcake's head.

"Veronica," she called back, "don't you see the signs?"

"Yes. But what does 'Quarreling not admitted' mean? And what is eff-foo-vess . . . ?" she asked slowly. "Wait, is that the bubbly stuff in soda?"

Missy said patiently, "I'm sorry, Veronica, but I'm afraid no one can come in for a while. The house and

Lightfoot have caught the Effluvia. It's very contagious. I don't want anyone else to get it."

She thought she could hear Veronica sigh. "I really can't come in?"

"No."

"Oh." Veronica scuffed her way back to the sidewalk.

Five minutes later, Missy heard pounding on the door. "Hey! What's a quarantine? Missy?"

Missy hurried into the hallway and saw Frankfort Freeforall with his face mashed up against the window.

"Let me in!" he called. "Please? School's out. I'm bored."

"I'm sorry," said Missy, and she explained about the Effluvia again. By the time she was done explaining, seven children were standing on the porch.

"Then can we play out here?" called Melody. "I haven't seen you for two days. I miss you."

Missy thought. "All right," she said at last.

Linden Pettigrew looked helplessly around the yard. "What are we supposed to do?"

Missy tapped her head with one finger.

"Use our imaginations?" shouted Linden.

"Exactly."

Missy spent the next hour watching the children invent a game called Gorilla Tag (she never figured out the rules) and answering the phone.

The first call was from Melody. Missy looked outside and saw that Melody had abandoned Gorilla Tag and was sitting forlornly on the porch with her phone.

"I need to talk to you," said Melody. "We have to give oral reports in school, and I *hate* talking in front of the class. I can't do it."

Now, most adults would suggest to Melody that on report day she should picture her classmates sitting in their underwear, but Missy knew that wouldn't make a bit of difference. "You can practice over the phone with me," she told Melody. "Then practice in front of your parents. Practice and practice until you know your report inside out and you're an expert and can walk into your classroom with confidence. I'll help you every step of the way."

"Over the phone?" asked Melody with a tremble in her voice. "Because I don't want to stand here on the porch and yell my report to you."

"Over the phone," Missy assured her.

Veronica's mother called next.

"Is everything all right over there?" she asked. "Veronica just came home in tears."

Missy explained once more about the Effluvia.

"Oh dear," said Mrs. Cupcake.

In a town as small as Little Spring Valley, news, especially the gossipy sort, spreads quickly. All afternoon and into the evening, Missy's phone rang. Several parents wanted to know if Missy needed anything, but Mr. Pepperpot said, "Is it true that Georgie won't be able to play at the upside-down house for . . . several weeks?" And Mrs. Treadupon asked, "Are you positive the Effluvia is contagious? Einstein does enjoy spending time at your house."

Missy fell into her bed that night, exhausted, and lay on her back looking up at Lightfoot, who was sleeping in the air, her tail dangling above Wag's head.

3

The Sticky-Fingers Cure

THERE WAS EXACTLY one apartment building in Little Spring Valley, and everyone was fascinated by it. It was five stories high, which made it the tallest building in town. And it had been built twenty-five years before, which made it the newest building in town. There had been a lot of grumbling when it was under construction.

"This isn't New York City. What do we need a skyscraper for?" Dean Bean had wanted to know.

When the five-story skyscraper was completed, people stared at it. They asked permission to take the elevator (the only elevator in town) to the roof for a bird's-eye view of Little Spring Valley. They marveled at the people who chose to live in a building with a lot of other families and an elevator.

Twenty-five years later, people had grown used to the apartment building. It sat at one end of Juniper Street. Sixteen families lived in it. One of those families was Louie Grubbermitts's. Louie was ten years old. He had two older sisters, Rachel and Elena, who were fourteen and sixteen, which made them teenagers. The apartment they lived in with their moms was cozy and tidy.

"As neat as a pin," Mama Tricia liked to say.

"A place for everything and everything in its place," Mama Eloise would add.

In the living room were two couches and three armchairs. Each was covered in a pleasant stripy fabric. By each chair was a small stand, and on each stand was a lamp. The lamps matched.

In the kitchen was a wooden table covered with a cheerful yellow cloth. The table was surrounded by five chairs with cheerful yellow cushions that, of course, matched the cloth. There were pegs on the walls for hanging things and drawers and cabinets for everything else. One day Mrs. Freeforall, who was visiting the Grubbermittses with her son, Frankfort, opened a drawer while looking for a napkin and exclaimed, "This is the tidiest drawer I have ever seen in my life!" and she wasn't exaggerating, as many adults do.

Now, you might think that a bedroom inhabited by two teenagers would be messy, but you would be wrong. The room shared by Rachel and Elena was so neat that their friends were afraid to sit down when they visited.

"We're used to sitting on hills of dirty clothes," said Edwina Nevermore.

"Did you know," added Zephyr Mason, "that my mother put a hamper in my brother's room, and he's so lazy he throws his clothes on *top* of it instead of opening the lid?"

"Well, you can sit right there," said Rachel, pointing to her bed, which was covered with a perfectly smooth checked spread and had none of her old dolls or stuffed animals on it. (The old dolls and animals were lined up on a shelf, each one exactly two inches from the next.)

"Or you can sit on my bed," said Elena.

But everyone was afraid to make wrinkles in all the smoothness.

The bedroom belonging to Mama Tricia and Mama Eloise was just as tidy as their daughters'.

And then there was Louie's room.

Luckily for Mama Tricia, Mama Eloise, Rachel, and Elena, Louie usually kept his door closed. Even so, Rachel shuddered each time she passed his room. Just knowing what was on the other side of the door made her feel slightly queasy. "Can't you clean things out once in a while?" she asked her brother one night.

"Clean out my collections?" Louie exclaimed. "But I *collected* my collections! I got all those things on purpose. Why would I throw them out?"

"You can't walk across your floor without stepping on something." She peered through his partially open door. "In fact, where *is* the floor? I can't even see it."

"I made a path," Louie replied with dignity. "Right there. See?"

Rachel followed her brother's finger. "I don't see a path."

"It's very narrow."

"You mean invisible?"

Louie shrugged. He gazed proudly around the room at his collection of bottle caps and soda tabs, and his collection of boards and nails, and his collection of bark and leaves, and his collection of newspapers and magazines. Most of these things were strewn across the floor. On his desk was an album exploding with stamps. On his chair was a box overflowing with coins. On his bed sat a rubber band ball so big, he thought it might set a record for having been made by a ten-year-old.

"Can you believe I found all those rubber bands just lying around?" he asked Rachel. "On the street, on the sidewalk. Some of them were in trash cans. People actually threw them away!"

"You've been going through *trash cans*?" shrieked Rachel. She slammed Louie's door shut and fled down the hall and into the living room. "Mama Tricia!" she said breathlessly. "Mama Eloise! Louie's rubber band ball—did you know he got some of the rubber bands out of the trash? The *trash*!"

Mama Tricia glanced at her wife and smiled. "He's quite a scavenger."

"Scavenging animals eat other animals," pronounced Rachel. "Even dead ones."

"He's more like a hobo," said Elena, who was perched on the couch between her moms. "He walks around town with a bulging trash bag. He's disgusting."

"Don't say that about your brother," said Mama Eloise.

"Well, he is."

"You could probably catch the plague in his room," added Rachel.

"Enough," replied Mama Tricia. But when Elena and Rachel went off to do their homework, she turned to Mama Eloise and said, "Perhaps we should have a look around Louie's room sometime."

"Isn't that an invasion of his privacy?"

"It sounds like his room might be turning into a health hazard."

～～～

The next morning, when Louie and his sisters left for school, Louie didn't bother to close the door to his room. His mothers stood at the threshold and looked in. "Anyway, I should collect his laundry," said Mama Eloise, as if she were continuing a conversation. She stepped into the room. "Goodness."

"It's messier than ever," said Mama Tricia. She wrinkled her nose. "What's that smell?"

Mama Eloise sniffed. "Old peanut butter?" she suggested. "Mold?"

"Maybe it's just all the leaves," said Mama Tricia, and sneezed.

Mama Eloise toed some of the leaves aside and bent down. "What's this?"

Mama Tricia peered over her shoulder. "It looks like a snakeskin."

Mama Eloise jumped backward and fell onto her bottom. "Are you sure there isn't a snake inside it?"

"Yes," said Mama Tricia, who wasn't sure at all, and hastily covered the skin with the leaves again. She watched the leaves for several moments to make sure they didn't rustle.

Louie's moms settled themselves gingerly on his bed. "Is this Louie's T-shirt?" asked Mama Eloise. She held up a shirt that had been crumpled into a ball on the pillow.

Mama Tricia was still watching the leaves on the floor. She turned to look at the shirt. "What's that a picture of? A sea turtle? I don't remember Louie getting a shirt with a turtle on it."

"Neither do I. I don't remember where that came from, either." Mama Eloise pointed to a clock on the bedside table. It was shaped like a racing car.

"Maybe it was in a goody bag at a birthday party?"

"Maybe. It's kind of fancy for a goody-bag item. And what about the shirt?"

"I suppose he might have traded with a friend."

"I suppose."

Mama Tricia stood up. "We'd better leave for work."

Louie's moms hustled out of the room and closed the door tightly behind them.

〰〰〰

Elena was in charge of watching Louie when he came home from school that afternoon. She never worried when he came home late, because the life of a scavenger is poky and slow. She didn't hear the elevator door open until almost five o'clock. A few moments later,

Louie burst into the apartment with his backpack and a plastic bag.

He was wearing a brand-new red-and-black baseball cap that read I ♥ NY over the bill.

The very first thing Elena said to her brother was not "Hi" or "How was school?" but "Where did you get that hat?"

Louie's face turned a faint shade of pink. Then he smiled broadly. "I just found it! Can you believe it?"

"No."

"Well, I did."

"Where? On some kid's head?"

Louie hummed under his breath. Then he squatted on the floor and opened the plastic bag.

"Do not open that thing in here!" cried Elena. "Take it to your room."

"But I want to show you what I found today. Look. Here's a dead oak leaf for my leaf collection. And here's a penny from 1951. It was just lying on the sidewalk. Plus I found seven more rubber bands. Oh, and this piece of wood has three holes in it that I'm pretty sure were made by a woodpecker. Isn't that cool?"

Despite herself, Elena leaned over and peered at the wood. "It is kind of cool," she admitted.

Louie was just reaching back into the bag when two things happened at once:

1. Mama Eloise walked through the door to the apartment.

2. A shout came from the girls' bedroom, and Rachel stomped into the living room with a red face.

"Hi, everybody!" said Mama Eloise cheerfully.

"Give it, Louie!" demanded Rachel. She held out her hand.

Mama Eloise frowned. "Rachel?"

Rachel glared at her brother. "I said, give it!"

Louie looked at her blankly.

Mama Eloise set her bags on the couch. "What's going on, Rachel? Please explain so that we can understand you."

"I'll show you instead." Rachel spun around and marched back to her room. Mama Eloise, Elena, and

Louie followed her in a line. Louie walked more slowly than the others, and by the time he'd dragged himself into his sisters' room, Rachel was standing by the shelves with her arms crossed. "That," she said. She pointed to the third shelf from the bottom.

"What am I looking at?" asked Mama Eloise.

"Stuffed animal, stuffed animal, doll," said Rachel, touching each item on the shelf, "stuffed animal, big empty space, doll."

Elena frowned. "Why is there an empty space?"

"Good question," replied Rachel. "Louie? Would you care to tell us?"

"No."

"If I go into your room, will I find a stuffed giraffe somewhere?"

"I don't know."

"You don't know if there's a giraffe in your room, or you don't know if I'll find it?"

When Louie didn't answer, Rachel flung open the door to his room.

Mama Eloise almost shrieked, "Watch out for snakes!" but stopped herself just in time.

"It's *right there!*" exclaimed Rachel. "Sitting in plain

sight. Poor Jerry Giraffe." She picked up the old giraffe and hugged it.

"Gosh," said Louie, "I wonder how he got in here."

Rachel turned to her mother. "He just went in our room and took it!"

Elena narrowed her eyes. "Hey, is that my seashell? The one I found in Florida?" She snatched a conch shell from the swirl of leaves and bark and bottle caps.

Louie snatched it back. "That's mine!"

"You're telling me you found this on the beach," said Elena.

"Um, yup."

"And then you wrote *Elena* inside it with pink nail polish?"

"Louie, this has to stop," said Mama Eloise. "Collections are fine, but you can't take things that belong to other people."

"But I thought maybe I would start collecting shells and stuffed animals." He paused to consider. "And hats and T-shirts."

"Well, find shells and stuffed animals that aren't in our room," said Rachel, and she stomped off, followed by Elena.

That night Louie's moms had a talk with him. They explained that it was wrong to take things that didn't belong to him.

"The stuff I find on the street doesn't belong to me," said Louie, wide-eyed, "until I put it in my bag. Then it does."

Mama Tricia sighed. "No. More. Pilfering," she said sternly.

But the next day Louie came home with a new baseball glove, and the day after that he came home with a large unopened candy bar. He was made to return each item to its owner, and Mama Tricia went along with him, which Louie found embarrassing. For several days after the candy bar incident, Louie came home with nothing more than rubber bands.

Then on Sunday morning Mama Eloise poked her head into Louie's room and let out a scream. "Louie! What's that on your pillow?"

It turned out it was a ferret, and it had been living in Louie's room for a day and a half.

"Whose ferret is it?" asked the moms when their hearts were beating normally again.

"Mine now," said Louie.

Elena poked her head into the room. "I'll bet that's Zelda. She belongs to Stephanie on the second floor."

"Stephanie is probably frantic with worry," said Mama Eloise.

Mama Tricia accompanied Louie and Zelda to Stephanie's apartment. When Stephanie opened her door, she gasped, then glared fiercely at Louie. "It was *you!*" she cried. "You took her!" She grabbed Zelda from Louie's arms, hugged her so tightly that Zelda let out a tiny squeak, and then glared at Louie once more before swiveling around and closing the door with her foot.

"She didn't even thank me!" exclaimed Louie, looking at the door.

"For stealing Zelda?" asked Mama Tricia, and shook her head.

Upstairs, Mama Eloise phoned Missy Piggle-Wiggle.

~~~~~

Winter or summer, weekends at the upside-down house were usually very busy for Missy. Her doorbell started ringing early, and children trooped in and out until it was suppertime and their parents called them to come home. The children wanted to play games and walk Wag and feed the animals in the barn and dig for pirate treasure in the yard if the ground wasn't frozen. But on this sad Sunday, the right-side-up upside-down house was silent, and two sorry signs hung outside.

Missy sat in an armchair in the parlor and watched Lightfoot float slowly across the room above her head. She peered through a window and saw Melody bundled up in a lawn chair in the yard, reading *Mary Poppins* and chewing on her hair. She watched the Freeforall children walk slowly down the sidewalk, stop, stare at the house, wave forlornly to Melody, and keep on going.

Missy's doorbell hadn't rung since the moment she had posted the signs. Her phone had rung, however. In fact, it rang more often than usual. Missy stared at it now, and it rang again.

"Hello?" said Missy.

"Hello?" replied an unfamiliar voice. "Is this Missy Piggle-Wiggle?"

"It is."

"Oh, good. My name is Eloise Grubbermitts."

"Ah. Louie's mom."

"Exactly. I'm also Elena and Rachel's mom."

"But you're calling about Louie, aren't you?"

"Well, yes. You see"—Eloise Grubbermitts chuckled—"things keep turning up in Louie's room that don't belong to him."

Missy frowned slightly. It was not as if the things had feet and had walked into his room on their own. "Hmm," she said. "How did they get there?"

"I suppose that Louie has, well, sticky fingers."

"Hmm," said Missy again. "How sticky are they?"

After a pause, Eloise said, "Sticky enough to pick up a neighbor's ferret."

"Good heavens."

"I know." Suddenly Eloise sounded as if she might cry. "It's actually a very big problem. At first he was just gathering things for his collections, but now he's taking things that belong to other people, and he doesn't seem to understand that this is wrong."

"Don't worry," said Missy soothingly. "I have just the cure. I'll leave it for you on the porch. Just follow the instructions in the bag."

~~~~~~

Eloise Grubbermitts was so desperate for help with Louie that she arrived at the right-side-up upside-down house just seconds after Missy had set the cure on the porch. Eloise hurried along the walk, looking curiously at the girl curled in a lawn chair reading a book, and snatched up the bag. "Thank you!" she shouted to Missy. "I hope you get well soon!"

Back at the apartment, Mama Eloise and Mama Tricia examined the jar that had been inside the paper bag. The label on it read SFC.

"SFC?" said Mama Tricia. "What does that mean?"

Mama Eloise shrugged. She opened the jar and peered inside. "It's some kind of powder." She sniffed. "It smells nice, sort of like cinnamon." She reached back in the bag and pulled out a slip of paper.

Sprinkle ½ teaspoon of Sticky-Fingers Cure on breakfast cereal. Repeat dose in two days if necessary.

"But what does it do exactly?" asked Mama Tricia.

"I suppose we'll find out."

~~~~~

The next morning Louie announced that he planned to go scavenging again after school.

"Scavenging, *not* pilfering," Mama Tricia reminded him.

Mama Eloise hurriedly sprinkled the SFC powder on Louie's cereal and handed him the bowl.

"Mmm. Cinnamony," said Louie, and he gobbled it up.

On the way to school that day, Louie found two rubber bands in the gutter, a soda tab at the edge of a garden, and the dusty wing of a moth. He placed them in his bag. In the hallway outside his classroom, he found a paper clip and decided to start a paper clip collection. Then he walked into the room and found a pen that wrote in three colors. The pen was sitting on Ashleigh Dalmatian's desk. In his head, Louie heard Mama Tricia say, "Scavenging, *not* pilfering," but he couldn't help himself. The pen would be perfect for keeping notes about his collections.

Louie picked up the pen and opened his bag. He tried to drop the pen inside but discovered that it was stuck to his hand. He shook his hand. The pen waggled back and forth but remained stuck. He shook his hand harder. The pen waggled faster.

"Hey! That's my pen!" cried Ashleigh, hurrying toward her desk.

Louie didn't know what to say.

Ashleigh hesitated. She was known in the fifth grade for being pleasant and polite and caring. "Did you want to borrow it?" she asked.

Louie nodded.

"Well, okay. You can use it until the bell rings. Then I need it back."

Louie, his face red, sat at his desk and tried to write with the pen. When the bell rang, Ashleigh said, "Could I please have my pen back now, Louie?"

"Um, okay." Louie used his left hand to yank at the pen in his right hand. The pen remained stuck. He held his hand toward Ashleigh. "Here," he said hopefully.

Ashleigh grasped the pen. She tugged it. She pulled it. She pulled so hard that she and Louie fell over. But the pen wouldn't come off Louie's hand.

"Huh," said Louie.

Their teacher clapped his hands. "Everyone in your seats, please."

Louie made his way wonderingly to his desk. Ashleigh glared at him.

~~~~~

At lunchtime, Louie, the pen still attached to his hand, glanced across the table at Rusty Goodenough's tray and saw a nice blue feather resting on a napkin. *I could start a feather collection,* Louie thought, and reached for it. It was very small, and Louie was sure Rusty wouldn't notice that it was gone.

Louie whisked the feather into his pocket. When he withdrew his hand, the feather was still in his palm, next to the pen.

"Hey, where's my feather?" cried Rusty. He looked at Louie's hand. "Give it back! I need that for my science project."

"Oh," said Louie. "I didn't know." He extended his hand to Rusty.

Rusty grabbed the feather. He tugged and tugged. "What did you do? Glue it to your hand?"

"No."

Louie spent the rest of school with the pen and the feather attached to his right hand. By the time he returned to his apartment that afternoon, a candy bar (the same kind he had been made to return several days earlier) was stuck to his left hand, along with a book and an iPhone. A pair of shorts was stuck to his chest, and a yo-yo was stuck to his cheek.

"What on earth?" exclaimed Rachel, who was in charge of her brother that day.

Louie tried to smile at her.

Suddenly Rachel laughed. "Those are things you stole, aren't they?"

"I was collecting, not stealing," said Louie, raising his chin.

At dinner that night he found that he couldn't hold a fork in his right hand, because of the pen and the feather, and he couldn't hold one in his left hand, because of the book and the iPhone.

"Would you like me to feed you?" asked Elena.

"No!" Louie asked Mama Tricia for some soup, which he drank through a straw, the yo-yo unspooling beside his face from time to time.

That night Mama Eloise looked at her wife and said, "Missy Piggle-Wiggle is certainly clever. Louie will be cured in no time."

But Louie found his habit difficult to break. By the end of the week, he looked like a walking rummage sale. His friends had little to say to him except, "Hey, that's my watch!" or "Is that my comic book?" or "That's mine! Give it back!"

"You can barely move!" Elena exclaimed to her brother on Friday. "In fact, I can barely see you. Where's your face?"

Louie didn't answer her. He knew he had a big problem. And like all the children in Little Spring Valley, he knew that the best way to solve a big problem was to talk to Missy Piggle-Wiggle. "I'm going outside," he called to Elena, and off he went to Missy's.

When he reached her house, he stood uncertainly on the sidewalk and stared at the right-side-up doors and windows and chimney. At last he made his way to the porch. He read the signs, then knocked on the door and called, "Missy? Are you in there? It's me, Louie. Can I talk to you?"

"If you don't mind a conversation through the door," replied Missy.

"No." Louie sighed. Then he said, "I have a big problem."

Missy looked at him through the window. "So I see."

"Can you help me?"

"Sometimes we have to help ourselves."

Louie thought about that. "I've tried. I told everybody they could have their things back, but my friends, um, aren't strong enough to pull them off."

"Maybe there's another solution," said Missy.

"And I have to think of it myself, don't I?" grumbled Louie. He turned around and clanked his way back home.

After dinner he knocked politely on his sisters' door. "I've learned my lesson," he told them. "I shouldn't have taken these things. They aren't mine. Can you please help me get them off? I'm hungry."

"Fine," said Rachel. She and Elena grasped a pair of sneakers and pulled.

"That doesn't really work," Louie told them. "Other people have tried. Maybe you could break them off."

"You can't return broken things to their owners."

Louie slumped into his room.

That night he lay uncomfortably in bed. He thought and thought about how he could release all the shoes and toys and books from his body. By the next morning, he had made a decision. As soon as breakfast was over, he took the elevator to the third floor and rang the bell at the apartment of a third grader named Sampson Checkers.

"Hi, Sammy," said Louie. Sampson began to back away from him. "Don't worry. I'm not going to take anything from you."

"You mean, anything *else*."

"Yes. That's why I'm here. I just wanted to say I'm sorry for taking your comic book."

"Are you going to give it back?"

Slowly Louie shook his head. "I want to. But I can't. It won't come off. I'm sorry."

Even though Zelda the ferret wasn't stuck to Louie, he stopped off at the next floor of the building on his way outside and rang Stephanie's bell. Stephanie opened the door holding Zelda, and she whisked her above her head and jumped backward.

"Don't worry," said Louie for the second time in three minutes. "I'm not going to take anything. I just wanted to apologize again. I'm sorry about what I did."

"Really? Well . . . thank you."

"You're welcome," Louie said, and realized he felt a bit better.

Outside on Juniper Street, Louie took inventory of the things that were clanking around on his body. He realized he had dozens of visits to make. In one block alone, he made three stops.

"Mr. Spectacle," he said, after waiting patiently in line in Harold's bookstore, "I'm very sorry I took your closed sign, but it was just hanging on your door and I really wanted it."

Harold didn't think this was much of an apology, but he said "That's all right" anyway.

On and on and on went Louie's apologies. He stopped in stores. He rang doorbells. He tracked down his friend Linden Pettigrew at basketball practice. He yelled an apology to Georgie Pepperpot since Georgie was too mad at Louie to open the door.

"I'M REALLY SORRY I TOOK YOUR SHOES!"

The door opened a crack. "You are? Thank you."

"Yes. I am. Are you still mad?"

"A little."

"Okay. I guess I would be, too."

It was after lunch when Louie walked tiredly up the steps to Ashleigh Dalmatian's house. "Ashleigh," he said, after she had let him inside, "I came to tell you that I'm sorry I took your pen."

Ashleigh nodded and looked longingly at the pen waggling around on Louie's crowded right hand. "It's kind of special. My aunt gave it to me for my birthday. She gave me a journal, too, and she said she thinks I can be a writer one day—which is what I want to be more than anything else! So those were my best birthday presents this year." She regarded Louie. He was standing stiffly by a chair, and he looked exhausted. "Can you sit down?" she asked.

"Not really." Louie turned around so she could see the board game and the football attached to his backside.

"Gosh. You must be really uncomfortable."

Louie stared at the floor. "You're worried about me after what I did?"

"I can't think only about myself. What's the point in that?"

Louie blinked. "I'm sorry," he said again. "I mean, *really* sorry. I didn't know the pen was special. I should have asked you before I took it."

And just like that, the pen dropped off Louie's palm and fell to the floor. "Hey!" he exclaimed.

Ashleigh dived for the pen. "Thanks, Louie!"

"You're welcome," he murmured in amazement.

At his next stop, which was Veronica Cupcake's house, Louie said, "Veronica, I'm sorry I took the picture you made. I don't even know why I took it, except that it was really pretty and—"

"You thought my picture was pretty?"

Louie nodded. "But I didn't think about how much it might mean to you. You probably wanted to show it to your parents."

Before Louie had even finished speaking, the picture had drifted off his shirt and floated to the floor.

"Thank you!" cried Veronica.

Suddenly Louie didn't feel tired. He continued his apologies, and at each stop another item unlatched itself. By the time he walked through the door to his apartment, the only things on his body were his clothes. His moms and his sisters looked at him in amazement. Louie smiled at them and then shrugged. "I'm going to go clean out my room," he announced.

Then, as so many parents in Little Spring Valley had done at one time or another, Mama Eloise picked up her phone and called Missy Piggle-Wiggle to say thank you.

4

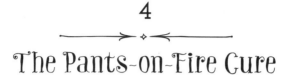

The Pants-on-Fire Cure

AT THE VERY edge of Little Spring Valley, on the other side of town from the elementary school, began a lane that wound far out into the countryside. Near the beginning of that lane, where the air smelled more like country than town but where neighbors could still see the houses on either side of them if they looked hard enough, was a rambling old home belonging to the Clavicles. It was the sort of country house with a wide porch, where the Clavicle aunts hung pots of bright red and pink flowers in the summer. There were gables on the roof, and windows poking out where you wouldn't expect them, and three staircases inside, and lots of hidey-holes for Almandine Clavicle, who was ten. The Clavicles were a largish family, and even so there were more bedrooms in the house than people to sleep in them.

Almandine liked to make lists, and she pasted them (every single one of them since her very first list, written when she was six) in a book she'd entitled *The Collected Lists of Almandine Clavicle*. That first list read:

My Pets

1. None

(Some of Almandine's lists were on the short side.)
A recent list read:

The People in My Family

1. Me, Almandine, 10
2. Mother, 40
3. Father, 41
4. Grandmother (Father's mother), 72
5. Grandfather (Father's father), 75
6. Nana (Mother's mother), 74
7. Auntie Adelaide (Mother's sister), 45

8. Auntie Columbia (Mother's brother's sister-in-law), 48

Almandine had made lists of the furniture in her room, her favorite names for dogs, the types of potatoes she had eaten, the colors of a zebra (1. Black, 2. White), the brands of all the sneakers she had ever worn, and on and on and on.

Mother and Father Clavicle thought Almandine was extraordinary.

"She's so precise," said her mother.

"She's so creative," said her father, although secretly he wondered about the zebra list.

The Clavicle household was quiet, and Almandine was sweet and obedient. Every day after school she came directly home, ate a snack with her grandparents, and settled down to do her homework. She sat at the desk in her sunny pink-and-yellow room and diligently filled out worksheets and wrote essays. Her report cards were filled with Bs.

"She's such a wonderfully above-average child," Auntie Adelaide commented to Auntie Columbia one night.

"And it's so nice that she always wants to be at home with us," replied Auntie Columbia. "She's never even been on a sleepover."

Almandine had once read a book called *Understood Betsy*, about a little girl named Betsy (of course) who lives, at least in the beginning of the story, with two older relatives who dote on her and who shelter her from the hardships of life. Then she moves to a farm to stay with different relatives, who expect Betsy to do everything for herself and even give her chores. At the end of the story, Betsy decides she likes these relatives better and wants to live with them. Almandine had been puzzled and didn't understand the point of the story. "It's a very strange tale," she had informed her teacher when she handed in her book report.

Almandine enjoyed her quiet life with all the grown-ups, but every now and then she did wish she had a friend. Sometimes she even dared to wish for a best friend. Most of her classmates had best friends. At the end of every school day, Almandine started off her walk home with six or seven other children who lived nearer to town, but she eventually finished off the walk along the lane all by herself. She would often stand for a few moments in front of the house next door to hers and look at the FOR SALE sign in the yard. The house had once been owned by the Minstrels, a very nice man and woman who were folk singers but who didn't have any children. They had moved away over a year earlier, and the house was still empty. The FOR SALE sign had become gray and lopsided. Almandine would feel lonely for a few moments, looking at the leaning sign and the empty house, but then she would step through her front door and the grandparents would hug her and give her a snack.

One afternoon Almandine was startled to find Nana waiting for her at the beginning of the lane.

"Is something wrong?" asked Almandine.

Nana smiled at her. "No. I have a surprise for you. Keep your eyes closed."

Almandine didn't like walking along the lane with her eyes closed, even if Nana had taken her hand and was leading the way. But she did so—slowly, in case there should be a rock or a snake in her path that Nana didn't see. At last Nana came to a stop, turned Almandine so that she was facing away from the road (as far as Almandine could tell), and said, "Open your eyes!"

Almandine opened her eyes and squinted in the sunshine. They were standing in front of the Minstrels' house. She glanced up at her grandmother. "What?"

"Don't you notice anything? Look around the yard."

"Oh!" exclaimed Almandine after a moment. "The for-sale sign is gone."

Nana smiled. "We're going to have new neighbors."

After her snack Almandine rushed to her room and began a list:

Things I Hope the New Neighbors Will Have

1. Children, three would be good
2. Dogs, five would be good
3. A trampoline
4. A girl exactly my age
5. Twin girls exactly my age
6. Someone who will be my best friend

Almandine knew this was a lot to hope for, but she couldn't help herself. She peppered her parents and aunts and grandparents with questions: When will the new people move in? Where are they from? Do they have any children?

Nobody knew the answers.

Every morning Almandine looked out her window first thing to see if a moving van had pulled into the driveway next door. Every afternoon she rushed home from school expecting to see the new neighbors lugging boxes and suitcases out of their car and up the steps of the porch. Finally, *finally*, after two weeks of waiting, Almandine ran along her lane after school, and there in the Minstrels' old yard were two cars, a moving van, a man, a woman, three children, and five people wearing BOHREN'S MOVERS jackets. Almandine stopped in her tracks and stared at all the activity. Eventually she noticed that one of the kids, a girl, was looking back at her from the porch.

The girl waved. "Hi!" she called.

"Hi." Almandine set her backpack down and started across the yard, feeling excited and shy.

"My name is Putney," said the girl. "Putney Cadwallader."

"I'm Almandine Clavicle. I live next door."

"What school do you go to?"

"There's only one here. Little Spring Valley Elementary. I'm in fifth grade."

"I'm in fifth grade, too!"

"Maybe we'll be in the same class," said Almandine, even though she privately thought this was too much to hope for.

Almandine got busy with her lists that evening:

Things the Cadwuh Cadd New Neighbors Have:

1. Three children
2. A girl exactly my age
3. Two dogs

Things the New Neighbors Do Not Have:

1. Five dogs
2. A trampoline
3. Twin girls exactly my age

Things the New Neighbors Might Have— I'm Not Sure Yet:

1. Someone who will be my best friend

Two mornings later, as the Cadwalladers were settling into their new home and new town, Almandine walked to Little Spring Valley Elementary with all three Cadwallader children—Putney; Joseph, who was eleven; and Benny, who was seven.

"I'm a girl sandwich," Putney announced. "My brothers are the bread."

"Do you play an instrument?" Joseph asked Almandine. Before she could answer, he went on. "We all do. Putney plays the guitar, Benny plays the piano, and I play the flute."

"We're a trio," added Benny.

"I don't play an instrument," said Almandine, who couldn't carry a tune and sounded like a cow when she tried to sing.

Benny patted her hand. "That's okay."

Two weeks went by before Almandine realized that she did in fact have a best friend, her first best friend ever. She and Putney were in the same class at school. They did their homework together in the afternoons. Sometimes Putney ate dinner at the Clavicles' house, and sometimes Almandine ate dinner at the Cadwalladers' house. Almandine and Putney were exactly the same size and could share clothes. They liked to read. They liked dogs. Almandine learned how to spell Putney's last name.

One night in November, Putney was at the Clavicles' having her third dinner with them. The Clavicles always ate in the dining room using their good china. They spread cloth napkins in their laps. This was why Putney liked dinner at Almandine's house. The Cadwalladers ate in their kitchen using paper plates and paper cups to avoid breakage. They used paper towels instead of napkins. Sometimes the dogs drooled under the table. This was why Almandine liked dinner at Putney's house.

On this particular evening, Grandmother wiped her mouth with a lace-edged flowered napkin and said, "Has anyone heard about the Winter Effluvia?"

"What's the Winter Effluvia?" asked Putney.

"It's a particular kind of flu," replied Auntie Adelaide.

"We only have it here in Little Spring Valley," added Almandine. "Luckily it doesn't come around very often."

"I heard that it's across town at the funny lady's house," said Mr. Clavicle.

"What funny lady?" asked Putney. There was so much about her new town that she didn't know.

"Missy Piggle-Wiggle," answered Almandine. "She lives in an upside-down house, only now it's right-side-up because of the flu."

"It's quarantined," added Nana with a shudder.

"Missy can cure problems," announced Almandine.

Putney looked from face to face as the story of Missy and her magic and the flu unfurled. At last she said, "My brothers and I are going to perform in the holiday program at school."

The conversation about the flu came to an end. All eyes turned toward Putney. "Perform?" repeated Mrs. Clavicle.

"On their musical instruments," said Almandine proudly.

"Oh, my," said Auntie Columbia. "All three of you play?"

"Piano, flute, and guitar. I play the guitar."

Grandmother's eyes shone. "And what will you be performing?"

"Two songs. The first—"

"Two!" exclaimed Grandfather. "Imagine."

"So talented," murmured Mr. Clavicle, who had put down his fork and stopped eating.

"The first," Putney began again, "will be 'Up on the Housetop.' The second will be 'Frosty the Snowman.' Benny wanted that one. And then I'm going to play a guitar solo. Probably a Beatles song."

The flu was forgotten. Missy was forgotten. Even Almandine was a little forgotten.

"You must bring your guitar over sometime and give us a private concert," Nana said to Putney.

Putney turned to Almandine. "Maybe I could play 'If I Had a Hammer' and you could sing along with me."

Almandine was familiar with the song all right, thanks to the Minstrels, but she hung her head because her entire family knew that her singing sounded like mooing. There was a little silence, and then Grandmother said brightly, "We'll be sure to attend the holiday program, Putney."

"Yes, all of us," added Auntie Adelaide.

"I'm going to be a snowflake in our class play," Almandine reminded her family.

"Lovely, dear," said Mr. Clavicle.

The next week report cards came out. "Straight Bs again," said Almandine with relief when she and her parents logged on to the website.

Putney got straight As. Luckily, the Clavicle adults didn't ask about her grades. But the next time Putney sat down around the fancy dining table and placed her napkin in her lap, she told Almandine's family that after Christmas she and her brothers were going to fly by themselves all the way to California to visit their grandparents. "We just found out about the trip," she said. "We're so excited."

"You're going by *yourselves*?" Almandine repeated. "Aren't you scared?"

"Oh, no. We've done it before."

"What? Flown, or visited your grandparents in California?"

"Both."

"My," said Mother.

The next evening, Almandine was seated around the Cadwalladers' table, eating macaroni and cheese from a paper plate, Harry the beagle drooling pleasantly on her ankles, when suddenly she found herself saying, "Next summer my friend is going on a trip down the Nile River."

"Really? Cool!" exclaimed Joseph.

"Yeah, cool," said Putney. "Which friend?"

"Um, you don't know her. Her name is . . . Candy."

"Candy. That's a funny name."

"She's going to go animal watching and see gorillas and pandas."

"On the Nile?" asked Mr. Cadwallader.

"I believe so," Almandine replied primly.

The *next* night, when Putney was at the Clavicles' again, she didn't even wait for the food to be served before she said, "Almandine told us about Candy's trip to Africa."

"Excuse me?" said Father.

"Who's Candy?" asked Grandmother.

"*You* know," said Almandine, sounding faintly cross.

Putney looked from face to face to face.

"My friend. Candy," said Almandine.

Mother frowned. "Do we know her? Who are her parents?"

"She's just . . . at school."

"She isn't in our class," spoke up Putney.

"So what? She's still going on a trip down the Nile. To see the pandas and jungle animals."

"That doesn't sound quite—" Grandfather began, but stopped himself. "Well, that will be some trip," he said after a moment.

Almandine looked thoughtful, then added, "And she's going all by herself."

Later that week, when the best friends were eating dinner at their own houses for once, Almandine suddenly announced to her family, "Guess what. Today during art, Mrs. Hambly said I made the best painting in the class, and she, um, hung it by the front entrance of school . . . so it's the first thing anyone sees when they walk through the door."

"Honey, how wonderful!" exclaimed Auntie Columbia.

"We'll have to drop by school so we can see it," said Father.

"I'll take a picture of it," said Nana.

"Well," said Almandine, "it might not be up for very long."

"Then we'll go first thing in the morning," said Father, smiling.

"On our way to work," added Mother.

"Oh, no," said Almandine. "It might have been taken

down already. It was just a sort of, um, one-day honor kind of thing."

"Odd," murmured Grandmother.

"But still it's an honor," said Mother.

~~~~~

Three miles away, in the right-side-up upside-down house, Missy Piggle-Wiggle stood at her front window, looking over the top edge of the quarantine sign, and sighed. Lester, who was sitting on the couch holding a lukewarm cup of coffee, glanced at her.

"Someone will be calling soon," Missy told him. "I sense a problem somewhere. Someone needs my help." She sighed again as Lightfoot floated out of the parlor and into the hallway, bobbing gently against the ceiling like a balloon. "No sign of the Effluvia letting up," she added, "although *I* still feel right as rain."

~~~~~

In the Clavicle home later that evening, the adults kissed Almandine good night one by one, and then gathered around the table in the dining room.

"There's no one at school named Candy," Father announced. "I've asked around."

"I'd be surprised if a painting by Almandine was hanging by the front door today," said Nana.

"Do you know what she told me after dinner?" asked Mother. "That on the way home from school today, she found a giant diamond on the sidewalk but that she left it where it was in case its owner came looking for it."

"She told *me*," said Auntie Adelaide, "that last year she found an injured dog and saved its life."

"Tall tales," said Grandfather. "Every single one of them."

"She's never lied before," said Mother.

"Well, it has to be stopped," said Father. "Who knows what lying could lead to. A life of crime."

"I hardly think she's a criminal," Mother replied. "But I'm not sure what to do about this."

"Punish her?" suggested Auntie Columbia weakly.

No one could bear the thought. Almandine had never before needed to be punished. The adults sat silently around the table until finally Mother said, "I suppose we could call Missy Piggle-Wiggle. That's what all the parents do when there's a problem. Tricia Grubber-mitts was telling me about the miracle Missy worked with Louie."

"And," added Nana, "Missy cured those insufferable Forthright children of their whining."

"I'll call her right now," said Mother.

When Missy's phone rang, she wasn't one bit surprised. "Ah," she said to Lester, "here's the call."

Almandine's mother introduced herself to Missy and inquired politely how the battle with the flu was going. Then, quite suddenly, she burst into tears and cried, "Our lovely Almandine has become a liar!"

"A liar. Goodness. When did this begin?"

Mother paused and thought. "I suppose it began shortly after Putney Cadwallader moved next door. She's Almandine's first real friend, and she's just lovely. So accomplished, too. She plays the guitar and she's very bright. And bold! She thinks nothing of hopping on a plane without her parents and traveling all the way to California. Why, our Almandine has never even been on a sleepover."

"Ah. I think I see the problem," said Missy.

"Really? Do you know Almandine?" Mother was

fairly certain that Almandine had never been to the upside-down house.

"I feel that I do," Missy replied cryptically.

"Well, what's wrong? What happened to her?"

"And I know just the cure," Missy continued.

In the background she could hear a voice, presumably the voice of Almandine's father, say, "We'll do anything."

"Do we give her pills? A tonic?" asked Mother.

"It's easier than that. A simple air freshener. Just hang it somewhere in your house and let it do its work."

"Our house is quite large," said Almandine's mother uncertainly.

"I'll give you two, then. Can someone pick them up tomorrow? I'll leave them on the porch."

When Missy had finished the call, she sat thoughtfully in a right-side-up chair for a few moments. Penelope flapped into the room. "Liar, liar, pants on fire!" she squawked.

Missy smiled. "But the problem isn't Almandine's," she told her.

The next morning Missy carried a small paper bag to the front door. Inside were two bars of something that looked like soap and smelled pleasantly like Christmas—pine and cinnamon and peppermint. Attached to each was a red ribbon for easy hanging. The air fresheners, which did not have labels, had come from the dark recesses of Missy's cabinet, where the cures were for things such as Judginess and Comparisonitis, cures that, in Missy's mind, were intended for use on parents, not children.

Ten minutes after Missy left the bag on the porch, Grandmother Clavicle picked it up, moving faster than usual in order to outrun the Effluvia, and drove the lovely-smelling fresheners back to the house in the country. She hung one in the dining room and one in the second-floor hallway.

She wondered what would happen next.

At first nothing at all happened except that the scent of peppermint made Almandine want a candy cane.

Then two days later, Mr. and Mrs. Clavicle were cleaning up the kitchen after dinner when Mr. Clavicle suddenly said, "Did you know that Ellie Cadwallader plays the guitar just like her daughter? Turns out she's Putney's music teacher."

Mrs. Clavicle handed him a dishcloth. "That house certainly attracts musicians."

"Ellie has even played professionally. I ran into her at the bank today, and she told me all the places where she's performed."

Almandine's mother tried to think of something interesting that *she* could mention.

"Imagine performing in New York, in Paris, in Vienna," her husband went on.

"Did I ever tell you about the time," began Mrs. Clavicle, "that I caught a five-pound fish?"

"When you were in second grade?"

"Well, yes."

Almandine's father lifted his head and sniffed. "I do like the scent of Missy's air freshener. I wonder what it's doing."

The day after that, Saturday, Mrs. Clavicle looked out the front door and caught sight of Putney's father raking a flower bed in his lawn. A box of tulip bulbs sat beside him. She hurried into the Cadwalladers' yard and looked approvingly at the bulbs.

"I do all the gardening myself," Mr. Cadwallader informed her. "Don't hold with gardening services." When Almandine's mother peered into the carton, he added, "There are a hundred and fifty bulbs in there. Next spring this yard will look like Holland."

"How lovely," said Mrs. Clavicle approvingly. She hurried home to report this to her husband. "The Cadwalladers' yard will be the showpiece of the neighborhood come spring! And Robinson does all the gardening himself."

"I could do our gardening if I had the time," said Mr. Clavicle.

"No. You couldn't. Remember the cactus? We barely even had to water it, and it died."

Over the next week the names Ellie and Robinson Cadwallader seemed to be mentioned frequently in the Clavicle home.

Ellie decorated Putney's house with the most tasteful lights Mr. Clavicle had ever seen.

Robinson brought over homemade Christmas cookies that were the best Mrs. Clavicle had ever eaten.

Ellie could make things with a needle and thread

that were fancier than anything Mr. Clavicle had seen in a store.

Robinson shoveled his own driveway after the first snowfall and announced that he didn't hold with plowing services any more than with gardening services.

And on and on and on.

After dinner one night, Almandine's father set out a chocolate torte he had picked up at the bakery on his way home from work. Mrs. Clavicle put a bite in her mouth and said, "Mmm."

"I know, I know. Robinson could probably make a better one," muttered Mr. Clavicle from the other end of the table.

"Dear, I said, 'Mmm.' I love this. Why are you bringing up Robinson?"

"Well, you did say you thought his cookies were good enough to get him on *The Great Baking Championship*."

"I was paying him a compliment."

"It sort of sounded like you think I can't bake."

"I have an idea!" said Grandmother brightly. "Why don't we leave the dishes for later and sing Christmas carols in the living room?"

Mrs. Clavicle glared at her husband. "No. I'm afraid amateur music won't do."

Almandine stared down at her plate. "I'm sorry I moo when I sing."

"Oh, no, darling! That isn't what I meant."

"What *did* you mean? We all know I moo. And anyway, Father, why do you care if you can't bake? You're the best storyteller I've ever heard." Almandine turned to her mother. "And you always recommend the best books. Your recommendations are even better than Ms. Porridge's." (Ms. Porridge was Almandine's teacher, the one who had suggested she read *Understood Betsy*.)

After Almandine went to bed that night, Mr. and Mrs. Clavicle sat by the Christmas tree, smelling pine.

"Is that the tree or Missy's air freshener?" asked Mrs. Clavicle.

Mr. Clavicle shrugged. There was a little silence before he said, "I know what you're thinking, dear. I'm thinking it myself."

"Then I'll say it straight-out. We've been comparing each other to Putney's parents, just like we compared Almandine to Putney."

"It doesn't feel very nice."

"Plus, what's the point?"

"I have an idea," said Mr. Clavicle, and he got out a piece of paper and a pen.

When Almandine awoke the next morning, she found something taped to her mirror. She pulled it off and crawled back in bed to read it. It was a list:

Things We Love About Our Daughter

1. She's the most cheerful person we know.
2. She's a hard worker.
3. She tries her best.
4. She secretly does nice things for people.
5. She's a good friend.
6. She's kind to animals.

The list went on for two pages and was slightly longer than the longest list Almandine had ever made. She read it through twice, then ran downstairs and hugged her parents. "Thank you," she said.

Suddenly she raised her head and sniffed the air. "What happened to Missy's freshener?" she asked. "I don't smell it anymore."

"Neither do I," said Mrs. Clavicle.

"Neither do I," said Mr. Clavicle.

Almandine ran into the dining room. "It's gone!" she exclaimed. "Only the ribbon is left." She ran upstairs. "This one's gone, too," she called.

"Oh dear," said Mr. Clavicle. "I hope Missy didn't expect us to return them."

"Well, anyway," added Mrs. Clavicle, "I think they did the trick."

Across town, Missy, who was tidying up her bedroom, suddenly sniffed the air. "Ah. Pine and cinnamon and peppermint. I believe the Clavicles have been cured," she said, and she plumped her pillow with satisfaction.

5

The Who's-the-Boss Cure

THE HOME BELONGING to the Cupcake family was small and tidy and, at least from the outside, cheerful. Bright yellow curtains hung in the downstairs windows, and bright blue curtains hung in the upstairs windows. In the spring tulips and daffodils poked out of the lawn, in the summer roses spilled from the gardens, in the autumn pumpkins lined the steps to the porch, and in the winter golden lights twinkled from the trees. Anyone passing by the house would say, "What a sweet home."

But if you paused there long enough, eventually

you might hear something like this from behind the sweet walls:

"I WANT TO WEAR MY PURPLE DRESS! YOU SAID I COULD!"

"I said that before I knew it was in the washing machine."

"BUT YOU *SAID* I COULD *WEAR* IT!"

"I made a mistake."

"BUT I WANT IT! I WANT IT, I WANT IT, I WANT IT!"

Or you might hear something like this:

"I'M NOT READY TO GO TO BED YET!"

"I'm sorry, but it's bedtime."

"BUT I'M NOT READY! I JUST SAID SO!"

"Veronica, it's eight o'clock."

"I DON'T CARE! I WANT TO STAY UP!"

Veronica Cupcake, who could be a perfectly nice little girl when she felt like it, lived in this house with her parents and her sister, Isobel, who was a senior in high school and practically another mother to Veronica. Isobel was ten when Veronica was born. When the Cupcake parents had brought Veronica home from the hospital, they held hands with Isobel and stared down at the baby lying peacefully in her crib.

"She's so sweet," said Mrs. Cupcake.

"She's an angel," said Mr. Cupcake.

"She's perfect," said Isobel.

Every minute of every day, the Cupcakes hovered around Veronica. At her slightest cry, they rushed to her side.

"Here's another toy," Isobel would say.

"I'll rock you," her mother would say.

"Let's change your shirt," her father would say, and hurry to the bureau overflowing with new clothes.

You would think that Veronica's first word might have been "yes" since people were always offering her wonderful things. "Do you want the hat with the flowers?" "Do you want to ride in your swing?" "Do you want your new stuffed teddy?"

Instead Veronica's first word was "no." And not just "no," but "NO!"

"Don't cry, Veronica. Do you want me to play house with you?"

"NO!"

"Oh dear. You aren't eating your supper. Do you want me to make you spaghetti?"

"NO!"

The next two words Veronica learned to say were "I want." They were followed by all sorts of other words, such as:

ice cream

your shoes

to go outside *right now*

a dog. No, not a stuffed dog, a real dog. A REAL DOG!

"She certainly does know her mind," said Mr. Cupcake one afternoon.

"Only three years old and already she has a sense of style," added Mrs. Cupcake.

The Cupcakes were having this conversation in the car on the way home from a department store in the city, where they had gone to buy Veronica some new pants. The trip had started off well because just as they were getting into the car that morning, Veronica had said, "I WANT CHEERIOS!" so Mr. Cupcake had hurried back inside and found the Cheerios and also a juice box, since you never knew what else Veronica might need, and need very loudly. Consequently, Veronica had been quiet all the way to the mall. But then the trip had fallen completely apart. As soon as they entered the Clothes Line and found the girls' department, Veronica had run to a rack of velvet dresses and proclaimed, "I WANT THE BLUE ONE!"

"But you don't need a dress. You need pants," Mrs. Cupcake had reminded her.

"NO! A DRESS!"

"The dresses are awfully expensive," said Mr. Cupcake.

"I WANT THE BLUE ONE!"

"You need pants."

"THE BLUE DRESS!"

Veronica's parents had looked at each other. In the end, Mr. Cupcake had said tiredly, "We'll get both," and the salesperson had packaged up the pants. Veronica had worn the new dress home over her old dress.

~~~~~~

One day when Veronica was four, her mother had said tiredly to her father at the end of a very long day, "You don't suppose Veronica's behavior could be our fault, do you?"

"Yes!" Isobel had shouted from the top of the stairs, where she'd been eavesdropping. She joined her parents in the living room. "My fault, too. We've spoiled her; all of us have."

"Oh no. She isn't spoiled," said Mr. Cupcake. "Is she?"

"How could such a beautiful little creature be spoiled?" added Mrs. Cupcake.

"Although we do give her everything she wants. Sometimes even before she asks for it," her father said, bunching up his eyebrows.

"I've been reading about child psychology," said Isobel, who had just entered high school, "and I believe that we have to start saying no to her."

"Oh, goodness," said both of the Cupcake parents.

"That won't go over well," added Mr. Cupcake.

"We have to say it at least once in a while," said Isobel.

"I suppose it couldn't hurt." Mrs. Cupcake spoke nervously, thinking of the scenes that were certain to follow.

The very next morning, when Isobel was getting ready for high school and Veronica was getting ready for preschool, Veronica opened her sister's door without knocking and said, "I want to take Mrs. Kitten to school with me today."

Mrs. Kitten was a stuffed orange cat that Isobel had been given on her first birthday. She was soft and worn, and both her tail and one button eye were hanging from her body by a single thread. Stuffing was leaking out around the base of her tail. "Oh no," said Isobel. "Mrs. Kitten is too delicate. She's very old. She might not survive the trip."

"BUT I WANT HER!"

"Nope. Sorry. She can't go to school with you." Isobel moved Mrs. Kitten from the bed to a bookshelf, out of Veronica's reach.

"I SAID I WANT HER!"

"I heard you, but the answer is no."

By this time Mr. and Mrs. Cupcake were standing in the doorway of Isobel's room, watching and listening. Privately, Mr. Cupcake was proud of the way his older daughter was standing her ground.

"I WANT TO SHOW MRS. KITTEN TO MY

FRIENDS!" Veronica began jumping up and down, trying to reach the cat. She stepped onto one of the lower shelves. "GIVE HER TO ME!"

"Here. Take this instead." Isobel handed her sister a photo of Mrs. Kitten and moved Mrs. Kitten to the very top of the bookshelf.

Veronica looked from the photo to the actual Mrs. Kitten, now high above her head. She plopped down on the bed and twirled a strand of her hair. She crossed her ankles and smiled prettily. "Isobel," she said, "you are the nicest sister in the world. The very nicest. Nobody else at my school has a sister as nice as you."

"Well, thank you," said Isobel in surprise. Then she glanced at her parents, pointed to her psychology book, and mouthed, "It works!"

"And since you are the nicest sister in the world," Veronica went on, "I really don't understand why you won't let me borrow Mrs. Kitten. Just for one morning. One little morning. I always tell my friends how nice and good you are. And how, um . . . What's that word that means you give people lots of things?"

"Generous?" suggested Isobel in a small voice.

"Yes! How generous you are. I always say that. I mean, when I can remember the word, I say it."

Isobel glanced at the aging and falling-apart Mrs. Kitten on top of the bookshelf. Then she looked again at her parents, who shrugged their shoulders.

"So please, generous sister, won't you let me borrow Mrs. Kitten just this one time? *Please?*"

Isobel reached for Mrs. Kitten. "Well, since you asked so nicely . . . I suppose. . . ."

Veronica snatched the cat from her sister so fast that the tail came close to falling off, and she ran downstairs.

"How do you think that went?" Isobel asked her parents.

"She did ask nicely," replied Mrs. Cupcake.

"She stopped shouting," Mr. Cupcake agreed.

~~~~~

Sure enough, people soon began commenting on what a lovely, polite, and extraordinarily complimentary child Veronica had become.

"She told me I make the best cookies in Little Spring Valley," said their neighbor Mr. Thorn one day, and he sent Veronica home with a dozen cookies in a polka-dot party bag.

"She told me my Bingo is the smartest dog she's ever met," said Mrs. Tremper, who lived next door to the Cupcakes and who let Veronica take Bingo home for a sleepover.

Mr. and Mrs. Cupcake had not forgotten what Isobel had said about the word *no*, however.

"We must remember to use it with Veronica," said her mother one rainy Saturday morning.

"And mean it," added her father.

Veronica wandered into the kitchen at that moment and said, "I want to go outside and play."

Mrs. Cupcake squared her shoulders. "No, darling. It's raining. Look out the window."

"But please, lovely mother, I want to go outdoors. I want to take a puddle walk."

Veronica turned smilingly to her father, but he said, "You heard your mother. What did she just say?"

"She said, 'Darling, it's raining.'"

"First she said no."

Veronica suddenly sat down on the floor. She stuck out her lower lip.

Her parents looked at each other in alarm. They put their hands over their ears and got ready for shouting.

Instead their daughter opened her eyes wide and said, "You don't want your Veronica to be sad, do you? Please let her go outside. Please? She's just a little girl."

Two minutes later, Veronica was taking her puddle walk.

~~~~~

Compliments and smiling prettily and delighting people with her lovely manners worked very well for Veronica when she was four, and pretty well when she was five, and sort of okay when she was six. By the time she was seven and growing tall and had learned to ride a two-wheeler and to read, she discovered that something had changed.

"Isobel, will you take me to the mall? I want to go to the toy store," she said one day.

Isobel was seventeen by then and could drive. She looked up from her computer and said, "Sorry, I can't. Mom and Dad have the cars."

"Then walk with me to Juniper Street. We'll go to the other toy store instead."

"What for?"

"A bubble machine."

"How are you going to pay for it?"

Veronica cocked her head to one side and smiled. "You'll buy it for me, won't you? Please? Pretty, pretty please?"

"Nope. I'm saving for a new phone."

"Then Mom will pay for it."

"She isn't here."

"You pay for it, and she can pay you back."

"I have a better idea," said Isobel. "I'll lend you the money, and *you* can pay me back."

"I don't have any money."

"Earn it."

"How am I supposed to earn money?"

"I don't know. Do jobs for Mom and Dad. Walk Bingo for Mrs. Tremper. You're a big girl. You'll think of something."

Veronica stood very still. "I want you to buy me a bubble machine."

"I know you do, but it isn't happening. I'll take a walk to Juniper Street with you, though."

Veronica glared at her sister. "You really won't buy me anything?"

"No!" Isobel laughed. "I told you. I'm saving my money."

~~~~~

It was exactly one week later that Veronica Cupcake had her first full-blown tantrum. It took place in A to Z Books.

"I just love walking into the bookstore," Veronica had announced gaily as she opened the door. She waited for the sneeze, and then she exclaimed, "Gesundheit!" She smiled up at her mother. "Isn't that funny? I said 'Gesundheit' to the sneezing door!"

"Yes, very funny," said her mother, even though Veronica said "Gesundheit" to the sneezing door every single time she opened it.

"Hi, Harold!" called Veronica. "I'm here for a visit. And to buy books. How are you today? I love your red hat. What are you doing?"

"Hello, Veronica. Hi, Mrs. Cupcake. I'm putting

together a package of books for Missy. A few things to take her mind off the flu."

"Would you like us to drop them off at her house?" asked Veronica's mother. "We'd be happy to."

Harold sighed dramatically. "That would be *wonderful*. The store is *so busy* today. Lots of Christmas shoppers."

Veronica smiled up at her mother again. "May I get five books?" she asked.

"You may get three. You'll be getting lots of Christmas presents very soon."

Veronica said nothing, and her mother suddenly felt anxious. She watched as her daughter walked slowly between the shelves of children's books. Veronica selected a copy of *How the Grinch Stole Christmas!* and tucked it under her arm.

"That's one book," said her mother.

Veronica stuck *A Tree Grows in Brooklyn* under her arm.

"Two," said her mother, "and I think that one's a bit old for you."

"I don't care. I like trees." Veronica pulled *Ramona the Pest* from a shelf.

"Three," said Mrs. Cupcake.

Veronica marched down another aisle and in the blink of an eye added *The Witches* and *The BFG* to her stack.

"Put two back," said her mother. "You have five books now. You choose which three to keep."

Veronica set all five books on the counter and looked at Harold. Harold looked at Mrs. Cupcake. His hands strayed toward his ears.

"I said three," Veronica's mother repeated.

"But I want these! I WANT THEM! I WANT THEM!" And in the blink of an eye, Veronica fell to the floor, rolled onto her back, and kicked her heels into the carpet. After that it was hard to understand what Veronica said. She shrieked so loudly that her voice grew hoarse. She flailed. When her mother tried to pick her up, Veronica kicked her in the ankle.

"Daddy, what's wrong with that girl?" a small boy asked.

Mrs. Cupcake looked helplessly at her daughter. Finally she said, "Darling, let's see if you get any of these books for Christmas. If you don't, we can come back and get them another time."

"That sounds reasonable," said Harold nervously.

"NO!" (That was Veronica, of course.)

"Then how about a compromise?" suggested her mother. "We'll get four instead of three or five."

"NO!"

Veronica's shrieks grew even louder, and the small boy pulled his hat down over his ears. Veronica kicked at a shelf and two books fell off.

"Okay," said Mrs. Cupcake in a hurry. She straightened up and said to Harold, "We'll take all of them."

Harold packaged up the books and handed them and the bag for Missy to Veronica's mother. Mrs. Cupcake grabbed Veronica by the wrist and hustled her outside.

Veronica sniffled all the way down Juniper Street. "Do you see how upset I am?" she asked. "I couldn't even say 'Gesundheit' to the door when we left."

Mrs. Cupcake didn't reply. When they reached Missy's house, she rang the bell and waited.

"We can't go in," Veronica reminded her. "It's quarmantined because of the effervescence."

But Mrs. Cupcake waited until Missy appeared in the window. Then she shouted, "We brought you some books from Harold!"

A smile came to Missy's face. "Lovely! Please leave them on the porch. I'm sorry I can't invite you in."

"I understand," said Mrs. Cupcake.

Missy thought Veronica's mother looked as though she wanted to say something more, but after a moment she turned slowly away and walked down the steps, Veronica skipping ahead of her.

Now, I wonder what that was about, Missy thought, and noticed a faint tingling at the tips of her fingers and toes. She watched as the Cupcakes made their way down the street. As soon as they were out of sight, Missy opened the door and reached for her present from Harold. She was smiling again.

~~~~~~

Mrs. Cupcake told her husband about the tantrum as soon as Veronica had gone to sleep that night.

"Perhaps it was an anomaly," replied Mr. Cupcake. "Perhaps she'll never have another one."

"Ha!" said Isobel from her room.

The next night the Cupcakes decided to go out for dinner. "We'd better go to Cocobelle's," said Isobel, "so Veronica can order from the children's menu."

At Cocobelle's, Veronica slid into a booth and announced, "I'm starving! I want mac and cheese."

Her father looked at the children's menu. He frowned. Then he looked at the rest of the menu. "Cocobelle's doesn't have mac and cheese. How about chicken fingers?"

"I said mac and cheese, not chicken fingers. I WANT MAC AND CHEESE!"

"Uh-oh," said Isobel.

"Please, oh please, dear mother and father, may I have mac and cheese?"

"It isn't on the menu," her father repeated in a careful low voice.

And with that, Veronica slid underneath the table and beat her feet on the floor.

"Veronica, get up! It's filthy down there!"

Veronica pounded her fists against the underside of the table. "I want mac and cheese! I WANT MAC AND CHEESE! I WANT MAC AND CHEESE!"

"That's it," said Isobel. "As soon as we get in the car, somebody had better phone Missy Piggle-Wiggle."

The Cupcakes left Cocobelle's in a big hurry, without even ordering. Isobel, her face flaming and her stomach growling, was aware of many pairs of eyes staring at them, and she heard one man say something about parents who couldn't control their children. As soon as they were in their car, Isobel sputtered, "Please, please call Missy now!"

Mrs. Cupcake drove the car while Veronica screeched in the back seat and Mr. Cupcake shouted into his phone, *"Is this Missy? This is Veronica's father! We have a little prob—"*

"Ask Isobel to stop by my house tomorrow on her way home from school," said Missy briskly. "I'll leave a parcel on the porch for you."

"But I haven't even told you—"

"I SAID I WANTED MAC AND CHEESE!" shrieked Veronica, and kicked the back of her mother's seat.

"No need," said Missy. Then she added kindly, "Don't worry. I see this sort of thing all the time."

The next afternoon Isobel ran all the way from her bus stop to the right-side-up upside-down house, even though it was snowing and very slippery. She grabbed the paper bag with her name on it from the steps; waved to Missy, who was watching from the front window; and slipped and slid down the street to her own house. She waited impatiently for her parents to come home from work. When they did, she thrust the bag at them and said, "Here. Quick! Give this to Veronica."

"But we don't even know what the cure *is*."

"I don't care. Whatever it is, just give it to her."

Mrs. Cupcake reached into the bag and pulled out a small box of candy. "Huh. Chocolates. And here are the directions. 'Give Veronica one chocolate after each meal.'"

"Now she gets *chocolates*?" said Isobel. "They'd better work."

"I wonder what they do," said Mrs. Cupcake.

"I don't care!" squawked Isobel.

The Cupcakes didn't have to wait long before trying Missy's cure. The next morning, which was Saturday, Mr. Cupcake said, "We need another string of lights for the Christmas tree. I'm going to run to Aunt Martha's General Store."

"Can I come with you?" asked Veronica.

"Have you had your candy?" Isobel asked.

Her sister looked surprised, but she said, "Yes, it was delicious. Thank you, dear sister." Then she put on her hat and coat.

At the store Mr. Cupcake wandered up and down the aisles.

"I'm bored," Veronica announced after a minute and a half.

"I'm sorry, but I haven't found what I need."

"Can I have new snow boots?"

"Nope. Sorry. We're here for tree lights."

And that was all it took. Veronica made her hands into fists, stretched her neck out like a goose, and emitted a screech. "I WANT—" she started to say.

Mr. Cupcake braced himself for a tantrum. Then he remembered Missy's chocolate, relaxed, and stood with his head cocked to one side, waiting to see what would happen.

What happened was that before his eyes, Veronica turned into a baby. Not a tiny baby, but a fifty-pound baby. A baby the exact size of Veronica Cupcake with her seven-year-old face, squalling on the floor, wearing an enormous yellow onesie and a lacy bonnet, and holding a rattle in one chubby fist.

"Wah-wah-wah!" wailed Veronica.

"Oh, my," a startled customer said to Mr. Cupcake. "What's wrong with your . . . baby?"

"Poor thing," added Aunt Martha, who had rushed to see what the commotion was about. "Maybe her diaper is wet."

Veronica wanted to say, "I'm too old to wear a diaper! I'm not a baby!" but all that came out of her mouth was, "Wah-wah-wah! Gooby-gobby-da-da-boo-boo."

Her father knelt next to her. "For heaven's sake," he said. "Veronica, the snow boots are expensive. If we wait until after the holidays, we can get them on sale."

Slowly Veronica's shrieking stopped. Then her sniffling stopped. The onesie and bonnet were replaced with her winter hat and coat.

"Goodness," said Aunt Martha, who had been watching in fascination. "Was all that fuss because you wanted boots? A big girl like you. I never."

"Did I just become a baby?" Veronica asked her father.

"I believe you did."

The storm that had begun on Friday continued all weekend, and by Sunday afternoon Little Spring Valley was soft and white and sparkling. Despite the snow and the excitement of the holidays, Veronica Cupcake had two more tantrums after her adventure at Aunt Martha's General Store. Mr. Cupcake, having witnessed that first tantrum, had thought it would put an end to things and that surely his daughter was cured. So he was disappointed to see Veronica squalling on the living floor that evening, rattle waving, after she had been told she couldn't eat a second candy cane. And he was even more disappointed to find her crawling around the kitchen the next morning, bawling because no one would agree to help her find her socks.

"Dad," Isobel whispered urgently to him. "Don't worry. I timed her tantrums and they're getting shorter."

That was a relief, but it was an even bigger relief when Veronica, recovered from her tantrum, announced that she was going to go to Missy's and build a snowman for her in order to cheer her up.

"What a lovely and thoughtful idea!" crowed Mrs. Cupcake. "Why, Missy will just—"

But Veronica was already out the door. A very

strange feeling had settled over her after the first tantrum, and she was restless and slightly crabby. She poked her way down the street to the right-side-up upside-down house, scuffing her boots in the snow and thinking about how unfair her entire life was. When she arrived at Missy's, she found Heavenly Earwig, Austin Forthright, Wareford Montpelier, and Linden Pettigrew already there. And what were they doing? They were rolling snow into large balls, getting ready to assemble a snowman.

Veronica came to a screeching stop at the end of the path to Missy's porch. "What do you think you're doing?" she demanded.

Austin looked up in surprise. "Making a snowman for Missy. To cheer her up."

"But that was my idea!" wailed Veronica.

"I guess we all had the same idea. Why don't you make another snowman?" Linden suggested. "Or maybe a snowdog."

Not one single person in the yard was surprised at what happened next. Veronica scrunched up her face and yelled, "YOU STOLE MY IDEA!" However, they were *very* surprised at what happened after that.

"Hey, look! She's— She's a *baby!*" exclaimed Linden.

Heavenly stared in such fascination that she lost her balance and fell forward onto the ball that was supposed to become the snowman's head.

"She's wearing a pink snowsuit!" exclaimed Austin.

"And booties!" cried Wareford.

"Is that a rattle?" asked Heavenly, getting up off the crushed head.

Veronica stopped shrieking. She hid the rattle behind her back. She looked in dismay at her friends, who were staring down at her.

Perhaps it was because Missy was watching the scene through her front window—who knows?—but not one of the children in the yard said anything further to Veronica, even though it was very tempting to call, "What a baby!" or "Wait here while I get you a bottle!" And Veronica had the presence of mind not to open her mouth, because she knew what would come out of it. Instead, she remained very still until she was standing up again and the snowsuit and rattle had disappeared. Then she said, "Sorry," and meant it.

Inside, Missy nodded slowly and smiled over at Lester on the couch.

Outside, Veronica and her friends peacefully made an entire snow family for Missy.

That night, as the Cupcakes sat around their Christmas tree looking at the lights and the ornaments, Veronica said thoughtfully, "You know, sometimes I act like a baby. But I'm not a baby. I'm seven!"

"You're a big girl," agreed her mother.

Veronica nodded.

"Old enough to have grown-up conversations," said Isobel. "Like I have with Mom and Dad."

Veronica nodded again. She said nothing more.

The rest of the Cupcakes felt as though they spent the next week holding their breaths, waiting for another tantrum. But Veronica didn't have a tantrum on Monday, or Tuesday, or even on Christmas, when they felt sure she would have a tantrum about *something*.

The tantrums were gone for good. The Cupcakes thanked Missy.

One day, years and years later, when Mrs. Cupcake was cleaning out the kitchen, she found a little box of old stale chocolates at the back of a cupboard. She tossed them out, saying, "Now, where on earth did these come from?"

6

The Chatterbox Cure

IN LITTLE SPRING Valley is a boy named Gabriel who lives on Juniper Street above the Snack Shoppe, which his parents own, and this is what it's like to have a conversation with him:

"You know what happened at lunch today?" Gabriel might say. "I was sitting with Linden and Frankfort and Louie and let me see, who else? Oh, I guess Almandine and that new girl Putney and maybe the twins, I don't know. It doesn't really matter to the story, but let me see. Okay, also Egmont and maybe two or three more people were there. That would be eleven or twelve altogether. That sounds about right."

"You said it isn't important to the story?"

"No, but, oh, I know! Rusty was there, too. And on my tray was a crumb. It looked like a crumb of cake or maybe a cookie. It could also have been a crumb of bread. I didn't want to waste it, because did you know that forty percent of all food is wasted every year? Actually, um, I guess that would mean that forty percent of all food is *always* wasted if that much is wasted every year, so I don't know why you have to *say* 'every year.' You could just say that forty percent of all food winds up being wasted. So I popped the crumb in my mouth, and guess what. It wasn't a crumb from a baked good at all. It was a teeny, tiny piece of meat."

"Ew! And did—"

"I wasn't expecting meat, so I was, like, really surprised. I said, 'Ew!'"

"That's what I just—"

"Plus the meat was cold, so I don't know how long it had been sitting on the tray. And, um, then I didn't know what to do next. I didn't want to be rude and spit it out, since there were about twelve people at the table. But I didn't want to swallow it, either, since it could have been really old meat. So finally I did spit it out.

Um, um, and later? I was thinking about the crumb, and I said to everyone, 'Remember when I had to spit out the meat? That was disgusting, right?' And, um, I think three people answered me. And then Linden said, 'It wasn't *that* disgusting.' But I know it was. *I* would have thought it was disgusting if somebody spit out food at the table, even if they spit it into a napkin, which I did, by the way."

Gabriel's full name was Gabriel Motormouth. He and his parents, Letti and Harley Motormouth, and his brother, Sven, who was a year older than Gabriel, had lived above the Snack Shoppe for five years, ever since they had opened it. Despite their last name, Gabriel was the only one in the family who actually *was* a motormouth. It would be an exaggeration to say that he talked twenty-four hours a day, because he didn't talk when he was asleep. Sometimes he talked when you might not expect it, though. For instance, when he was watching a movie or when he was at the dentist. At home, he had perfected the art of talking while brushing his teeth. Through the bathroom door, he would yell, "Ing cashe ayone ish ondering, I sfished to a new bran of toofpashe. It tashe kine of like, um, shpearmit if oo mished orange wif it or maybe, no, more like if oo mished fruit shalad wif it. Shven? Do oo hear me? Do oo wanna try the toofpashe? I'll leave it here onna counter, and oo can tell me what it tashe like to oo!"

The rest of the Motormouths were exhausted by Gabriel's chatter. They were befuddled by it, too.

"He certainly seems to like the sound of his own voice," Letti had remarked more than once.

"Always has," Harley would reply.

When Gabriel was three, he had announced that he would prefer to be called Gabe. And so all through pre-school and kindergarten, his classmates had dutifully called him Gabe. But by the end of first grade, they had decided on a different nickname for him: Gabby. Gabriel didn't seem to care. "Remember when Rusty wanted to be called Red, so we all called him Red for a while, but then he changed his mind and asked to be called Rusty again? That was funny. I mean, a little weird, but funny, too, and like he just couldn't make up his mind. Um, yesterday? When my mom was ordering supplies for the restaurant? She phoned this one company and said, 'Send five cartons of napkins, please. No, send six. No, wait, five.' She couldn't make up her mind!"

Sven and the Motormouth parents spent a lot of time trying to get a word in edgewise around Gabriel. It wasn't easy, since Gabriel was around a lot. He enjoyed sitting in the Snack Shoppe after school and on weekends, talking to the customers. He talked to anyone who entered the restaurant, whether he knew the person or had never seen him or her before. "Hey there, Mr. Thorn! Look at this. Look at the sole of my sneaker. It has a hole in it that's shaped exactly like a piece of pie. See? Well, I guess it could just be a triangle, but I think it looks like a piece of pie. Um, did you notice that we now offer lemon meringue pie in addition to our usual pies? Did you ever get a hole like this on the bottom of your shoe? This will be the first time I'll have to get new shoes due to a hole shaped like a serving of pie. In the past I've mostly had to get new shoes because I outgrew the old ones. And once I lost my shoes. That was on an airplane. Can you believe it? I put them under the seat in front of me with a lot of other stuff, and at the end of the trip they were gone and I had to exit the aircraft in my sock feet."

When Sven wasn't in school, he tried to be wherever Gabby wasn't. "So," he would say casually, stuffing his hands in his pockets and looking as though he couldn't care less about his brother's answer, "are you going to hang out in the restaurant this afternoon?"

"I guess. I think I might do my homework there. I want to see if Mr. Thorn will come in. The last time I sat down at his table, he gave me six pieces of gum. SIX! And I hadn't even said anything yet."

At this, Sven mentally clapped the side of his head and thought, *Gum! Why didn't I ever think of giving Gabby a giant wad of chewing gum?*

"Also, yesterday," Gabby continued, "Ms. Porridge came in." (Ms. Porridge was his teacher.) "You know what she ordered? She ordered a vegetable sandwich, hold the eggplant, and then she said, 'No, wait. I think I'd like the tofu wrap.' And then she said, 'No, wait, let's go back to the veggies, hold the eggplant.'"

Gabby paused, and Sven hoped this was the end of the story. He was relieved when Gabby drew in a breath and said, "Anyway, it was fun to see Ms. Porridge so I think I'll go downstairs again."

"Great!" exclaimed Sven before his brother could re-open his mouth. "Guess I'll stay up here today."

"What are you going to do?"

"Just my homework."

"I might stay up here, too."

"Or I might go to the restaurant," said Sven hastily.

In the end Sven went to the Snack Shoppe and Gabby followed him, so then Sven decided to go for a walk. Luckily, Gabby had in fact found Ms. Porridge in the restaurant, and when Sven slipped out the door, Gabby was sitting across from his teacher happily listing all the cats he had ever known.

Sven wandered up and down Juniper Street for a while. Snow was falling, and the sounds of shoppers talking and calling to one another, and the sounds of car horns and truck tires and jingling bells, were muted and seemed far away. Sven breathed in deeply. He left Juniper Street, walked as far as his school, and then turned and started for home.

He had tipped his head back and was catching snowflakes on his tongue, listening to the silence, when he heard a voice cry, "There you are! I was wondering where you had gone." Gabby was running toward him. "Did you hear that we might get NINE inches of snow?

Ms. Porridge said we'll probably have a snow day tomorrow! Remember last year, when we had twelve snow days?"

"Yup," said Sven. "We had so many that—"

"*Twelve.* I think that was an all-time record. I didn't like having to go to school for extra days at the end of the year, but what can you do? If we have a snow day tomorrow, I'm going to sleep late. Or wait, no, maybe I'll get up extra early so I can make full use of the day. I wonder when we'll hear for sure that school is closed. I hope it's tonight so then we can fall asleep already knowing the good news. . . ."

Sven was wearing a ski cap. Now he took it off, slipped a pair of earmuffs out of his pocket, put them on, and tugged the cap back on over them. "Cold," he said, even though Gabby wasn't listening to him.

Sven and his parents always kept earmuffs handy. "They don't drown out the sound of Gabby's voice as well as cotton balls do," Letti Motormouth had once remarked, "but they're more comfortable."

"Better than nothing," her husband had said.

The snow day was announced that evening just as the Motormouth parents were closing up the Snack Shoppe. Gabby came flying downstairs with the news. "It's closed! It's closed! School is closed tomorrow."

Harley shut his eyes briefly. "You'll probably want to play outdoors a lot, then. Snowmen and sledding and all."

"Or indoors! Or I could help out here!"

"I expect things will be pretty slow tomorrow," remarked his mother. Then she added, "Maybe you could stay upstairs and do something *quiet*. You know, take advantage of your unexpected vacation to just, oh, draw or make Christmas presents for your grandparents."

"Good idea," said Harley.

"What should I make for them? Remember last year, when I made picture frames? The macaroni kind of fell off, but I think they liked the frames anyway. Remember when Beaufort Crumpet made Christmas ornaments out of salt dough and his dog, Dottie, ate two of the ornaments and puked in the kitchen? Maybe I'll make ornaments for Nannie and Grandma, and Popsicle-stick boxes for Poppy and Granddad. We won't have to worry about the salt dough, since we don't have a dog." Gabby hurried back upstairs, talking all the while, even though he had to shout over his shoulder to be sure his parents could hear him.

The snow day came and went. Gabby made two ornaments and two boxes. The next morning the sun was shining. The plows had come during the night to clear the streets and had piled up small mountains of snow all over Little Spring Valley.

"Boy, those piles will be good for sledding," said Gabby. "You know, whoosh, whoosh, whoosh! Flying along like racing cars. I hope I get a racing car for Christmas. Not a real one, of course, but a remote control one that I can zoom around the house in winter and around the playground in summer. I asked my parents fourteen times for a racing car so far. I might mention it again tonight."

Gabby was walking to school with Louie Grubbermitts. Sven was wearing his earmuffs and walking twenty feet ahead of them.

"If you get a racing car," said Louie, "can—"

"Last year I asked for Monopoly and I got Sorry! *and* Monopoly. Oh, um, and my father got six pairs of socks.

Six socks, six socks. That's kind of a tongue twister. Also, it kind of sounds like 'ticktock.'"

Louie stopped listening. Sven picked up his pace and jogged the rest of the way to school. He was thinking that it was about time he talked with his parents.

~~~~~

Christmas came and went. Gabby got a racing car, and Sven got the bubble-gum-making kit he had asked for at the last minute. Vacation flew by, and finally it was New Year's Eve. Late in the day Gabby was deeply involved in creating an obstacle course for his car. He talked to himself the entire time. "Under the bed and around the chair, down the hallway and back. I'll make a bridge here out of, um, Legos. Oh, hi, Sven. Want to help me with—"

"Here, have some gum!" Sven handed his brother a large wad of homemade bubble gum and raced downstairs to the restaurant. No customers were there. His parents were sitting at one of the tables, sipping coffee and not talking. They looked up warily when Sven entered.

"Where's your brother?" asked Letti.

"Upstairs. And I just gave him gum. He can't talk."
Letti and Harley breathed sighs of relief and went back
to their coffee. "But *I* need to talk to you," said Sven.

"Anything wrong?" asked his father.

"Well, it's just that I never *get* to talk to you." His
parents nodded sadly. "I didn't get to tell you what I did
on the snow day. I didn't tell you that Mr. Mandible said
I should be taking private art lessons."

"Oh!" said Harley.

"That's wonderful," said Letti.

"I didn't tell you about my idea for a new sandwich
to put on the menu," Sven went on. "And do you know
why?"

Harley nodded again. "Yes."

"We don't even get to talk to *each other*," Letti added,
turning to her husband.

"Can't you make Gabby stop talking?" asked Sven.

"How?" said his father.

"We've tried Quiet Hour and the no-talking game
and even paying him not to talk," said Letti.

"And gum," added Sven glumly.

"Nothing works for long," said Harley.

The three Motormouths sighed in unison.

At last Letti said, "Well, let's talk now. It's the perfect opportunity."

So Sven and his parents had a long, peaceful talk. But they still had no idea what to do about Gabby.

~~~~~

Three days later vacation ended and school started again.

"Do you know what resolution I decided on?" Gabby exclaimed to Sven the moment they woke up. "Remember, I was deciding between helping out more in the restaurant and talking up more in class. Then I added on some other possibilities."

"Was one of them talking up less at home?" asked Sven.

Gabby laughed. "No! Why would I want to do that?"

That morning Gabby and Louie walked to school together as usual. Louie was wearing new earmuffs that Mama Tricia had bought for him at Aunt Martha's. "So finally I decided that I'll talk up more in class," Gabby announced, even though Louie had not mentioned anything at all about resolutions. "That should please

Ms. Porridge. It will let her know I pay attention to her. And that I care about what she says."

"My New Year's resolution—"

"I plan to put my resolution into effect today," Gabby went on.

And he did. During reading he gave a five-minute answer to the question, "Who is the main character in *Mrs. Frisby and the Rats of NIMH?*"

Louie leaned across the aisle and whispered to Putney, "I could have answered that in two seconds."

During history Gabby went on at length about his favorite mayors, even though Ms. Porridge had asked about crops in the New World.

Then came science class.

"Finally!" Louie whispered to Putney. "Only half an hour until recess." He thought fondly of his earmuffs. He planned to put them on first thing, even before his coat.

"As you know," said Ms. Porridge, "for the next few weeks we'll be studying endangered species."

Louie looked continually at the clock. The hands ticked on and on toward 11:30. At last there were just five minutes to go. And that was when it happened.

"Does anyone know," began Ms. Porridge, "how many endangered species there are in the world?"

Gabby shot his arm in the air. "Ooh! Ooh! I don't know how many there are, but I was just wondering what would happen if *people* became an endangered species. Like, if we were wiped out by aliens and slowly cats took over the planet. There would just be more and more and more and more cats. Oh, hey! Maybe that's where the idea for that book came from. *Millions of Cats.* Remember that one? My mom used to read it to my brother and me. . . ."

Gabby talked about *Millions of Cats* for a while, which made him remember a book called *Caps for Sale*, which made him remark that, for some reason, everyone in his family preferred earmuffs to caps.

Louie checked the clock: 11:27.

". . . that it would be very hard for dogs to become an endangered species," Gabby was now saying, "because people love dogs so much and also dogs protect people, which would make people want to protect dogs. Dogs aren't like scorpions, creatures that are scary to a lot of people. . . ."

11:29.

". . . and my favorite breed of dog is the chow, which I think is actually called the chow chow, and it's my favorite because it has not only a blue tongue, but blue gums and lips. It looks like it's been eating a grape Popsicle. You can't say that about any other kind of dog. . . ."

The next time Louie looked at the clock, it read 11:31.

He nudged Putney and pointed at the clock.

"I know!" she said in a loud whisper. "It's *after* eleven thirty."

At the front of the room, Ms. Porridge had stood up from her desk and was hovering over Gabriel.

". . . once ate three Popsicles, and my dad said I would get sick, but I only had a little stomachache. . . ."

"Gabr—" began Ms. Porridge a few moments later, when Gabby paused for breath.

". . . this crumb of meat on my tray . . ."

"Eleven forty!" Putney said to Louie.

It was almost 11:50 by the time Gabby wound down, and Ms. Porridge loudly and hastily announced that it was time for recess and for everyone to hurry and put on their coats and go outside.

"Yeah, for ten minutes," Louie muttered. Earmuffs

in place, he ran to the playground. The first person he saw was Sven, who was bouncing a basketball. Louie ran to him and grabbed the ball away.

"Hey!" cried Sven. Then he added, "How come you guys are so late?"

"Because of your brother! He wouldn't stop talking!"

Sven grabbed the ball back. "Well, that isn't my fault."

"I know. Sorry."

Putney and Almandine joined Louie. "Can't you do something about Gabby?" Almandine asked Sven. "Please?"

"What do you want me to do?"

Putney regarded him. "Just. Make. Him. Stop."

~~~~~~

That afternoon no one would walk home with Gabby, not even Louie, even though he lived directly across Juniper Street from him. And not even his own brother. Sven sat in the school library reading a book until he was certain Gabby was at home. When he finally reached the Snack Shoppe, he peered through the window, saw no sign of his brother, and went quietly inside.

"There you are!" cried Gabriel, leaping out from behind the counter. Sven jumped, but before he could say anything, Gabby went on, "Hey, who's that sitting over there by the window? I didn't notice him before. He doesn't look familiar. He must be new here. Or maybe he's a tourist. Or someone on a long trip."

Gabby hurried across the restaurant and sat down at the man's table. "Welcome to our establishment," he began. "I'm Gabriel Motormouth. My parents own the Snack Shoppe. May I recommend something for you? A lot of people like the wraps. We have meat ones and vegetable ones. Are you vegetarian, by any chance? Or maybe you're vegan. We have vegan choices, too."

"I already ordered—"

"Oh, look. Here comes my dad. Is that your hamburger? Oh, it is!" he said as Harley set the burger down in front of the man. "That's a good choice. I guess you're not vegan or vegetarian."

The man nodded at Gabby and sat politely waiting for him to leave, or at least stop talking, so he could start eating.

"In school we're learning about endangered species," Gabby went on. "Not that anything on your plate is endangered." (The man turned pale.) "And do you know what I said in class today? I said, 'What would happen if people became endangered and cats ruled the earth?'"

The man looked longingly at his burger. He reached for a fry but realized Gabby was nowhere near finished, so put his hand back in his lap. Ten minutes later he said, "Excuse me, would you mind if I started—"

". . . a crumb on my tray," Gabby was saying.

"I'm actually in a bit of a rush."

". . . and it was meat!"

Gabby was talking about the nine inches of snow and the day off from school when the man finally picked up his hamburger. He bit into it.

"It's cold," he muttered.

"Well, why did you wait so long to start eating it?"

The man glared at Gabby, then looked around the restaurant and held up his finger.

Harley hurried to the table. "Sir?" he said.

"I'm afraid my burger has gotten cold."

Harley glanced at his son. "My apologies," he said. "I'll get you another. On the house."

"No, no. That's quite all right." The man had pushed his chair back. "I'll just, I'll . . . Have a good day!" he said, and fled while he was still putting on his coat.

"Gabby, how long were you talking to—? Never mind," said Harley.

In a quiet moment that evening, Sven crept downstairs to the Snack Shoppe and told his parents what had happened in Gabby's class that day.

Harley mentioned the customer who had left without eating, or paying.

"What *are* we going to do?" wailed Letti, putting her head in her hands.

"Didn't the Grubbermitts call Missy Piggle-Wiggle for help with Louie?" asked Sven.

"That's right! They did!" exclaimed Letti, and she snatched up her phone and dialed Eloise.

Sven listened to his mother's end of the conversation. What he heard was: "You did? . . . It was? . . . He didn't mind? . . . *Completely* cured? . . . Thank you so much." Letti ended the call and immediately dialed Missy's number. When she ended *that* call, she said,

"I'm to pick up the cure tomorrow and administer it to Gabby in the afternoon."

Not one of the Motormouths asked what the cure was. They just put on their earmuffs, trundled up the stairs, went to bed, and in the morning found that they had all slept deeply.

~~~~~~

When the phone had rung at the right-side-up upside-down house the evening before, Missy was just ending a call with Melody Flowers. Melody, who tended to worry, had been saying, "Isn't the Effluvia over yet? It's been weeks."

"Sometimes it takes a while. Lester still isn't himself," Missy replied. "Neither is Lightfoot."

"Are you worried?"

Missy considered the question. Because she made it a policy not to lie to children, she said cautiously, "A little."

"And what about you? How do you feel?"

"Still right as rain. Don't worry about *me*."

Poor Mrs. Motormouth called then, so Melody hurried off the phone, saying, "I love you, Missy."

What Missy found most unbelievable about her conversation with Gabby's mother was how long it had taken for her to call. Missy had been living in Little Spring Valley for some time by then, and Gabby had been gabby for as long as she'd known him. Missy already had the perfect cure set and ready to go. It was just a matter of putting it in a bag and leaving it on the porch in the morning.

~~~~~

"It says, 'Give to Gabby as soon as he comes home from school,'" Letti told her husband when she rushed back into the Snack Shoppe that morning, a note from Missy in her hand.

"Give what to him?"

Letti held out a little tin. "There's only one thing in here. It looks like a peppermint."

Harley peered inside the box. "Okay. And then what?"

"I guess we just wait to see what happens."

Needless to say, Letti Motormouth gave her younger son the candy the moment he rushed into the Snack Shoppe after school that day.

"Mmm. Tasty," he said. "Thanks, Mom."

Letti waited for a torrent of words from Gabby, but instead she found *herself* saying, "Is it good? You know, peppermint is really my favorite flavor. Well, that and orange. When I was a little girl, I used to beg my mother to buy orange soda, but she said it would rot my teeth, so we only got orange soda for a treat. Well, sometimes grape soda, but mostly orange. Generally, we just drank milk or water. And the milk was skim, which I didn't like, since it had a bluish hue to it. Somewhere along the line, I developed a taste for coffee, and then I forgot all about grape soda, or really any soda."

"Mom?" said Gabby, who was staring at his mother with very large dark eyes, like a nervous cat.

"You know, your father likes his coffee now and then," Letti continued, "but he doesn't put either milk or sugar in it, so I suppose it's healthier than what I drink. I just can't stand the taste of black coffee. . . ."

"Remember," said Gabby suddenly, "the time *Sven* tried cof—"

". . . course, your father had that experience with . . ."

Gabby, still wide-eyed, fled upstairs.

"Sven?" he called. "Sven, are you here?"

Sven appeared in the doorway to the bedroom. "Hey, there you are!" he exclaimed. "I was wondering where you'd got to. Look outside; it started to rain. Who said anything about rain this afternoon? I wanted to shoot baskets at the playground. I guess I'll just have to wait. Or maybe I could *try* playing in the rain. I've seen people playing ball in the rain. I just need to find my old poncho. It's probably in the closet. I hope Mom doesn't make us clean out the closet this spring. There's nothing worse than when she and Dad start talking about spring-cleaning. It is the most boring . . ."

Gabby put his hands over his ears. Talk about boring. Why was his brother going on and on about ponchos and cleaning closets? Did he need to say *every*thing that came into his head?

Apparently he did. And so did Gabby's parents. They chattered and talked nonstop. Later, when Gabby went downstairs, cautiously poked his head into the restaurant, and asked Mrs. Porridge, who was enjoying a scone at a table by the window, about his math homework, Mrs. Porridge said, "You know, I must not have been very clear about the assignment, because I've already gotten e-mails from Putney and Louie. Oh, and let me see, also from Almandine. I think everyone mistook the 5 I wrote on the board for a 6. That certainly wouldn't have made sense! My sloppy handwriting. And here I'm constantly after you kids to be more careful."

"But that wasn't—" Gabby began.

"My third-grade teacher would be appalled if she could see how I write sometimes. She made us copy numbers and letters over and over and over and over. Sometimes forty times each. Or fifty."

Gabby, his question still unanswered, walked slowly back upstairs.

~~~~~

At school the next day, Gabby found that his classmates not only talked all the time, but they also all talked at the *same* time. His head began to ache. He put his hands over his ears. "Excuse me!" he called during a discussion about tigers. "Excuse me!" But no one heard him.

At recess, standing alone by a tree, the only place where he could find some quiet, Frankfort Freeforall broke the silence by dashing across the playground to

him and shouting, "Hey, we missed you yesterday. Where were you? I can't believe you didn't come! It was so much fun."

Gabby stared blankly at him. His hands gravitated toward his ears. But he couldn't help saying, "What was so much fun?"

"The hoops party. You know, Linden's basketball birthday party. He tried about ten times to invite you, but you just kept talking about owls. And some other stuff I've forgotten. Seeds, maybe. And a flat tire on a delivery truck. Anyway, there was a basketball coach at the party and he gave us tips about free throws. I scored five baskets and got a prize! Boy, you sure missed a good party."

Gabby vaguely remembered Linden trying to talk to him. He remembered more vividly that he himself had nattered on and on about the calls of various owls and had gone into great depth about an argument he and Sven had had over the sound a barn owl makes. And now he had missed Linden's party.

After school Gabby rushed home, through the Snack Shoppe, which was as noisy as an airport waiting room because everyone *there* was talking, too, and upstairs, where he lay on the couch in the living room and hoped Sven wouldn't come home. There were so many things he had wanted to say that day—for instance, about the bumblebee population. And just at that moment, he wanted to say to his mother, "I have a headache and I need a hug," but he knew that if he went back to the restaurant, he wouldn't be able to get a word in edgewise. At breakfast that morning, his entire family had talked about fleas for fourteen minutes.

Gabby didn't say a single thing for the rest of the day, and he wasn't sure his family even noticed as they jabbered on and on about so many dull topics that Gabby lost count.

It was during science class the next day, when all his classmates and Mrs. Porridge were talking, shouting even, about endangered species, that Gabby timidly uncovered his ears and raised his hand. Ms. Porridge stopped talking and looked at him. Gabby's classmates stopped talking and covered their own ears.

"Yes?" said Ms. Porridge, and she winced.

"There's a kind of bear, the Asian black bear," said

Gabby, "which is also called the moon bear, and I read that it's considered 'vulnerable.' It's in danger of becoming extinct." He folded his hands and looked around the room.

Louie raised his eyebrows.

For a moment everyone was silent.

"Part of the problem is deforestation," said Ms. Porridge.

Putney raised her hand. "What's deforestation?"

Gabby realized he didn't know the answer, so he looked intently at his teacher. And then a nice conversation unfolded, just the way conversations are supposed to unfold, with one person talking and the others listening, one person asking a question, and one other person answering.

Louie and Gabby walked home that afternoon, and when they reached Juniper Street, Gabby called, "See you tomorrow, Louie!"

"See you tomorrow, Gabe!"

Gabriel walked into the restaurant and wordlessly gave his mother a hug. She hugged him back. "How was school?" she asked.

"Fine. Really good, actually. Anything happen at the restaurant?"

~~~~~

Around the corner at the right-side-up upside-down house, Missy said to Lightfoot, who was bobbing along the ceiling in the kitchen, "Ah! I think the peppermint drop worked," and she went back to the book she was reading.

7

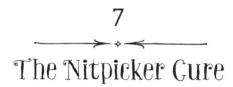

The Nitpicker Cure

ON A BRIGHT day that felt more like April than the middle of January, Missy Piggle-Wiggle stepped out the back door into the farmyard and stood in her boots in the snow, breathing deeply. "Ahh, just like spring," she remarked over her shoulder to Penelope.

Penelope was perched on a chair at the kitchen table. "Do not wait; don't hesitate!" she sang, bouncing up and down. "Call five-five-five-two-two-three-oh, and see your dentist now. Say good-bye to cavities!"

Missy frowned. "Did you hear me?" she asked. "I said it feels like spring today."

"Order your sandwiches from the Snack Shoppe. Find us on Juniper Street or find us online. We deliver!"

Missy felt her spirits sag. For the past few days, Penelope had done nothing but quote from jingles and commercials. It was impossible to have a conversation with her. "I'm afraid she's finally come down with the flu," Missy had said to Harold the night before. What a long, dreary winter this had been.

But, she reminded herself, in just a few months spring would arrive. Warren and Evelyn Goose would be watching over goslings again, Missy could ride Trotsky in the field, and best of all the Effluvia would vanish—she was certain of it. The house would turn upside down, and children would be ringing the doorbell and running through the rooms making a great lovely mess.

At that moment, though, spring seemed very far away.

Missy returned to the kitchen and set her snowy boots on a mat by the door. "I think I have cabin fever," she remarked to Lester, who was resting his chin on one front hoof and slowly stirring a cup of lukewarm coffee.

The phone rang then, and Missy dived for it. "Hello? Hello?"

"Hi, Missy, it's me," said Melody's voice. "I don't suppose I can come over yet."

"No, I'm sorry. Nothing has changed. I miss you!"

"I miss you, too. I have a question. What's a nitpicker?"

"A nitpicker?"

"Yes. Tulip was over yesterday, and after she left I heard my mother say to my father, 'Tulip certainly has become a nitpicker.'"

Missy had a feeling she might soon be getting a phone call from one of the Goodenough parents. "What do *you* think a nitpicker is?" she asked Melody.

"I think it might be a person who criticizes every little thing, even things you think are nice. Tulip doesn't whine. And she's not mean. It's just that she's always like, 'Hmm, you have a *green* bedspread now?' and 'Huh, your hair ribbon is, well, yesterday it was tied all perfectly and now . . .' and '*That's* your new shirt? I don't think it's the best style for you.' Are those the things one friend says to another?"

"Have you talked to Tulip about this?" asked Missy.

"I sort of tried to, and you know what she said? She said, 'I was just trying to *help* you.' But it didn't really feel like help. I wish I could come over so I could talk to you in person."

"So do I." Missy heard a knock at the door then, but since Penelope no longer announced who had arrived, she had to hurry to the front and look out the window. She wasn't surprised to see Rusty Goodenough standing on the porch next to the quarantine sign. "We'll talk more tonight," Missy said to Melody. She set her phone down as Rusty's knock turned to pounding.

"Rusty!" she called. "I still can't let you in."

"Are you sure?"

"Yes."

"Are you positive?"

"Yes."

"Are you absolutely positive?"

"Rusty."

"Well, can I talk to you from out here?"

"Of course."

Rusty plopped down on the porch floor, even though it was wet with slushy snow. "My sister is driving me crazy!" he shouted in to Missy. "She criticizes every-thing I do. *Everything.* She says I don't make my bed right, and I'm too loud, and I walk funny, and I fold my nap-kin wrong, and I also spread the peanut butter wrong. Why does she even care about those things? If she doesn't like the way I make my bed, she should stop looking in my room."

"I agree," said Missy.

"Well, what should I *do* about it? Oh, hi, Linden. Where did you come from?"

Missy peered through the window again and saw that Linden Pettigrew was standing on the steps behind Rusty.

"I could hear you shouting from all the way over at my house," said Linden. "Do you want to go sledding?"

"Missy, I'm going sledding with Linden. See you later!"

"Come back anytime," replied Missy. She looked up at Lightfoot, who was drifting along above her head. "There will almost certainly be a phone call from the Goodenoughs by the end of the weekend," she told her.

Across Little Spring Valley, Helene Goodenough, mother of Tulip and Rusty, sat on the couch in the living room and paged through Tulip's baby book. She looked at photo after photo of her dear, sweet daughter in the lovely days before she could talk. There was Tulip hugging her father around his neck; Tulip with oatmeal smeared over her face and the tray of her high chair, grinning a grin that showed off her newest teeth; Tulip reaching out her hand to pat their neighbor's dog.

Helene read some of the entries she had made in the book:

Tulip is an angel.

Tulip loved every moment of Barbara's birthday party!

Tulip was a trooper on a five-hour car ride.

Helene sighed and set the book down. She recalled the previous day's car ride to Juniper Street. In less than five *minutes*, Tulip had suggested that her parents take the car to the car wash, had remarked that Rusty's sock had a hole in it, and had very pleasantly noted that Almandine's parents always bought the good kind of peanut butter.

"What is the good kind?" Helene had asked wearily.

"The kind with the elephant on the jar. It's creamier

than the creamy kind we've been getting." Then she added, "Mom, when did you get those earrings?"

"Last week." When Tulip didn't say anything, Helene added, "Do you like them?"

"Yes. It's just that they're kind of small and hard to see. I mean, you really have to *look* for them. It's like, 'Oh, *there* they are, behind all your hair.' And they're such nice earrings, you wouldn't want to miss them."

"Hey, Tulip," said Rusty, from beside his sister in the back seat, "did you ever think that maybe—"

"I can see the top of your underwear," interrupted Tulip. "About an inch of it. Mom, did you get Rusty new underwear? I think it's too big for him."

Mrs. Goodenough found a parking spot on Juniper Street and edged into it. "You're supposed to be closer to the curb," said Tulip.

Helene pursed her lips, even though she wanted very much to ask her daughter when she had gotten her driver's license. After a moment she said, "Why don't you two go off to the library while I run errands? We'll meet back at the car in forty-five minutes."

"Gosh, look at the window of Aunt Martha's. That wreath is shedding needles everywhere," commented Tulip. "I don't know why they haven't taken it down."

Helene decided that her first stop that day would be for a cup of coffee at Bean's. She hurried inside and sat at a table by herself, sipping her coffee and enjoying the nice, peaceful restaurant. Afterward, she went to the shoe repair shop to pick up Tulip's good shoes, to Aunt Martha's for thread and wrapping paper, and up and down the street until it was time to meet Rusty and Tulip at the car.

"Mom, you're late. You were gone forty-eight minutes," Tulip greeted her. She was leaning against the car. "Boy, this is dirty," she said, turning to run her finger through the grit on one of the hubcaps.

"Well, it's hard to keep it clean in the winter with all the slush and sand." Mrs. Goodenough unlocked the car. "Where's your brother?"

"He's even later than you. Doesn't anyone listen around here? Oh, Mom. I'm sorry. I should help you with those." She took some of the packages from her mother's arms.

"Why, thank you," said Helene in surprise.

Tulip peered into the box containing her shoes. "Is this what you asked the repair guy to do?"

"Put on new soles? Yes."

"But he put on *white* soles. Oh, well. I guess I can wear them anyway."

~~~~~~

Now Helene sighed and put away her daughter's baby book. When exactly had Tulip become so nitpicky? It had happened recently, she realized, but slowly enough so that it seemed the nitpickiness had been going on forever. She looked at her watch. Tulip was at Samantha Tickle's house and had said she'd be home in time for dinner. Helene was just thinking that she had about another two hours of peace when the front door opened and in walked Tulip, saying, "Hey, the door squeaks."

"You're home early," replied her mother.

"Yeah. I don't know. Samantha got into a really bad mood and said maybe we should work on our project separately."

"I wonder what put her in a bad mood."

Tulip shrugged. "We were at the table with our

poster board and markers, and I was saying how *we* try to keep our kitchen floor from getting all yellow, and she just sat there for a minute, and then finally she said maybe I should work on my posters at home and she would work on hers at her house. Oh, well. My posters will look better with our markers anyway. Hers kind of have dried-up tips." Tulip sat on the couch next to her mother. "You know, if your blouse was just a little bit darker, it would match your scarf exactly."

"Well, I don't have a darker blouse."

"I'm just saying."

"Why don't you go upstairs and work on the posters in your room?"

Tulip shrugged. "Okay." She got to her feet. "Funny, I never noticed that."

"What?" asked her mother warily.

"The edge of the rug is starting to curl up." Tulip took a wide step over the curl, as if the rug might bite her, and ran to her room.

That evening while Helene and her husband were preparing dinner, she poked her head out of the kitchen, looked around, saw no sign of her children downstairs, and ducked back inside. She opened her mouth to complain to her husband, Marcel, about Tulip, but suddenly Marcel set down the bowl he'd been holding, slapped his hands on the counter, and burst out, "What on earth are we going to do?"

"About Tulip?"

"Yes! She's driving me crazy. Isn't she driving you crazy?"

Helene slumped into a chair. "The rug is curling up, the Tickles' kitchen floor is yellowing, my earrings are too small," she recited. "Rusty's sock has a hole; I bought the wrong kind of peanut butter."

"My glasses frames are too round," said Marcel, "there's a nick in the wallpaper, the toothpaste cap doesn't close all the way, she can smell the garbage."

"Maybe she's just become very, very observant," ventured Helene.

"Attentive to detail," agreed Marcel.

"That must be a good thing. Right?"

They returned to the salad they were arranging. After a few moments, Marcel said, "We're just making excuses for her."

Helene sighed. She didn't know it, but it was the sixty-fourth time she had sighed that day. "Tulip is so *polite* when she says these things. Have you noticed? She doesn't say, 'Mom, those are horrible earrings' or 'Why can't you ever buy the right peanut butter?'"

"And yet," said Marcel, "somehow we feel criticized."

"Exactly."

Fifteen minutes later the four Goodenoughs sat down to dinner.

"How come you got this kind of napkin?" Tulip asked her father, who had been to the grocery store that afternoon. "Was something wrong with the other ones?"

Mrs. Goodenough served the roast chicken. "You left the skin on?" said Tulip.

"May I please have the bread?" asked Rusty.

Tulip passed it to him, saying, "Gosh, your T-shirt is getting so thin."

"I don't care. It's my favorite. It's thin because I wear it all the time."

"I have an idea," said Marcel a few minutes later. "Why don't you kids finish your dinner in the TV room?"

"Really?" said Rusty. "We can eat in there? Thanks!"

When their children had left the table, Helene and Marcel stared at each other, wide-eyed. "My heavens," said Helene.

"I can't take this any longer," said Marcel.

"Should we call Missy? She did such a wonderful job with Rusty when he was spying on everyone."

"I suppose so. But I'm not sure this is really a problem."

"If it isn't a problem, why do we feel so awful?"

Marcel picked up his phone and called Missy.

At the right-side-up upside-down house, Missy was enjoying an evening with her animals, even though Penelope was reciting an annoying commercial about a pillow and Lester was napping and Lightfoot was bobbing her way from room to room. When the phone rang, Missy said to Wag, "I imagine that's the Goodenoughs. They're calling sooner than I thought they would." She looked at her phone. "Yup. It's Tulip's father." She settled onto the couch next to Lester, and Wag hopped in her lap.

"Hello?" said Missy. "Mr. Goodenough?"

"Hello," Marcel replied. He wanted to be polite and start off with some small talk, but instead he found himself saying, "It's terrible! Tulip has become the worst nitpicker! She criticizes everything. Every. Little. Thing."

Missy heard Helene say in the background, "She's driving her friends away!"

"This has to stop!"

"What did we do wrong?"

"Nitpickiness," Missy began calmly, "is fairly common. Don't worry. You wouldn't believe how often I get calls about it."

"Is there a cure?" asked Marcel.

"Absolutely. It takes a few days, but it's very effective. I'll leave the cure on the porch for you. You can pick it up first thing tomorrow."

"Couldn't I come over tonight? We want to get started right away."

An hour later, Mr. and Mrs. Goodenough were in their bedroom with the door closed, huddled over the small red box that had been left for them by Missy. Helene peered at the lid. The word *Nitpickiness* was scrawled in fancy gold script. "Did you ask Missy for instructions?" she said to her husband.

"She yelled through the door that they were in the box."

Helene lifted the lid and removed a slip of paper. The box was divided into three sections, with a tiny brass plate in each. The plates read LEVEL 1, LEVEL 2, and LEVEL 3, and each section contained a single pink tablet. She unfolded the paper. "'Give tablets exactly one day apart, starting with the Level 1 tablet at breakfast tomorrow morning,'" she read.

"And?" said Marcel.

"And that's it."

"But what's supposed to happen?"

"I guess we'll have to wait and see."

The next morning Tulip took the tablet along with her vitamins. Her parents watched her closely.

"Why are you staring at me?" she asked. Then she frowned. "What's this green stuff in the eggs?"

"Parsley," her father replied.

"Ooh, fancy!" said Rusty.

But Tulip frowned. "I don't like green stuff in my food. It looks like mold."

"You like grapes," said Rusty.

"Grapes *are* green. They don't have green stuff *in*— Hey!" Tulip stared at her plate. "The green stuff's gone!"

"It's *parsley*," said her brother, "not green stuff." Then he leaned over for a closer look. "It *is* gone!"

"How did that happen?" asked Tulip. She picked through the eggs to make sure a stray flake of parsley wasn't hiding somewhere, and then she cleaned her plate.

Later that morning, as the Goodenoughs sat in their living room with books and newspapers, Tulip stared moodily out the window and remarked, "We're the only people on the street whose Christmas lights are still up."

It was on the tip of her father's tongue to say, "Well, why don't you go outside and take them down?" when he realized that the little fir tree by the driveway was bare. "What happened to the tree?" he asked instead. "The lights are gone." He opened the front door and stood on the porch. "The lights around the windows are gone, too."

"I'll bet someone stole them," said Rusty.

"But I just saw them!" exclaimed Tulip. She hurried to the closet under the stairs and hauled out the box the lights had been stored in. "They're in here!" she exclaimed. "All neatly bundled up."

"What on earth?" said Marcel.

"First my eggs, then the lights. How *did* that happen?" asked Tulip.

Her parents raised their eyebrows at each other. Then Mrs. Goodenough said sadly, "I kind of wanted to leave the lights up for another week. I hate to see all the decorations come down."

"You do?" Tulip replied. "I didn't know that."

~~~~~

"What a weird day this has been," said Rusty over dinner that evening.

"I think it's been great!" exclaimed Tulip.

Her parents exchanged another glance. Her mother was thinking, *Well, of course she does. Everything she complained about was magically reversed.*

"The lights are gone, and they were *so* embarrassing," said Tulip. "And those horrible yellow apples Mom bought changed to red."

"I like yellow apples," remarked Rusty.

"Plus, all I had to say was what a mess your room was and it cleaned itself up!"

"That was okay, except that now I can't find anything."

"Not my problem," chirped Tulip. She glanced across the dining room. "There's a dead fly on the windowsill!" Before she could add, "Doesn't anyone ever clean up around here?" the fly disappeared. "I guess I have magical powers," she said. "I've kind of been thinking that all day. Watch this." She turned her attention to the offensive nick in the wallpaper and said, "This room would sure look a lot better if that nick got fixed."

The wallpaper smoothed itself out. "There was a nick?" said Rusty. "I didn't see any nick."

"What do you care? Your room is clean."

"I didn't *ask* for it to be cleaned up. And I can't find my homework. What am I going to do? I'm supposed to hand it in tomorrow."

That night, after Tulip and Rusty had gone to bed, their parents sat in the living room and shook their heads.

"What kind of lesson is this teaching Tulip?" asked Marcel.

"I have no idea. She complains about something and—poof—she gets her way."

"Maybe we should call Missy."

"No. Not yet. Missy always seems to know what she's doing. Let's give Tulip the second pill and see what happens."

On Monday morning Tulip pranced down the stairs and into the kitchen. "What a lovely day!" she exclaimed.

Rusty, who was already seated at the table and was sprinkling parsley flakes on his eggs just to make a point, looked out the window and said, "It's raining. And it's practically as dark as night."

"Oh, well," said Tulip gaily.

"You're in a happy mood," remarked her father.

"I just have a feeling it's going to be a very good day."

"That's because for some reason you keep getting your way," muttered Rusty. He still couldn't find his homework, and furthermore, he wanted a yellow apple.

The Goodenoughs sat at the table with their eggs and toast. After a while Tulip set down her fork and watched her father.

"Yes?" he said.

"Dad, you eat so slowly. You take, like, one bite per minute."

Mr. Goodenough was just about to say this was good for his digestion when his hand started shoveling food in his mouth so fast that the fork turned into a blur. His plate was clean in a matter of seconds.

Tulip stared at him. "Wow. I've never seen you eat like that before. It's like you're normal."

But poor Mr. Goodenough put one hand over his stomach and the other over his mouth and let out a long, loud belch.

"Cool!" said Rusty. "I didn't know grown-ups could do that."

Mrs. Goodenough, however, looked alarmed. "Marcel? Are you all right?"

He groaned. "I already have heartburn. I think I'll go lie down for a while. Can you call the office and tell them I'll be late?"

Rusty glared at his sister. "See what you did?"

"Well, gosh, I didn't know *that* would happen."

On the way to school, Tulip told Rusty to hurry up. "No," he said, "I don't—" But suddenly his feet were hurtling him along the sidewalk, and he slipped in a puddle of slush and crash-landed on a snowbank. He stood up and faced his sister angrily. "Look what you made me do! Now my library book is all wet. I'll have to pay a fine."

"I'm sorry," said Tulip, who looked much more awed than she did sorry. And in fact, the morning, as far as Tulip was concerned, was quite awesome. She pointed out to Samantha that her clothes were covered in cat fur, and the fur disappeared immediately. Tulip was pleased, but Samantha looked embarrassed.

She mentioned to Egmont Dolittle that he smelled like a wet dog.

"That's what happens when you walk a dog in the rain," Egmont informed her. "And anyway, it isn't nice to point out things like that."

But the wet dog smell went away, and Tulip felt satisfied.

It was during recess, which was held in the gym because of the rain, that trouble occurred. Melody and

Samantha were standing under a basketball net, deep in conversation. Melody kept patting the French braids in her hair, and Samantha was turning Melody's head from side to side.

"What's going on?" asked Tulip.

Samantha and Melody looked at each other warily.

"We're discussing Melody's hair," Samantha said after a moment.

"It's finally long enough for braids!" exclaimed Melody. "I've been waiting and waiting for this. Now I can do anything with my hair. Braids, ponytails. I can put it up or let it hang loose. I can even—"

"What's that?" said Tulip, squinting. She leaned forward and plucked something from the end of one of Melody's braids. "Huh. A little piece of food. Your hair is too long now, Melody. You should get it cut."

"But I just grew it out! It took forever!" She paused. "What?" she said when she saw the expression on Samantha's face. "What's wrong?"

"Uh-oh. Um, your hair . . ." Samantha's voice trailed off.

Melody reached for one of her braids and felt only the fabric of her sweatshirt. She patted her head. She felt a helmet of short hair and let out a shriek. "My hair! My hair!"

"It's so cute!" cried Tulip.

"I don't care. It isn't what I wanted. And anyway, it's none of your business what I do with my hair."

"Call Missy. She'll help you," said Samantha. She took Melody by the elbow and led her to the principal's office to use the phone. Before they left the gym, Samantha turned around and glared at Tulip.

Missy knew what to do, and by the time Melody had hung up the phone, her hair had been restored to the French braids. But neither Melody nor Samantha spoke to Tulip for the rest of the day.

"This is so unfair!" Tulip kept exclaiming as she hurried home behind her silent friends that afternoon. "All I said was you should cut your hair, and now you won't even talk to me."

At last Melody exclaimed, "Cut your own hair!" and ran ahead, arm in arm with Samantha.

The news of Melody and her hair spread quickly, and by dinnertime Helene and Marcel had heard all about what happened.

"Do you really think we should give her the last

pill?" Marcel whispered to his wife. "It was one thing when she could change *things*. Now she's changing *people*."

"Missy always knows best," Helene replied loyally.

~~~~

Tulip went off to school the next day with the Level 3 pill in her stomach and new mittens on her hands. She was surprised to find Melody and Samantha waiting for her outside school. "I thought you guys were mad at me," she said.

Melody shrugged. Samantha reached for one of Tulip's hands. "New mittens? Hmm."

"What?" said Tulip.

"They're just a little babyish, that's all. You should wear gloves."

"Mittens keep your hands warmer than—" Tulip started to say, but before she could finish the sentence, her mittens had changed to a pair of gloves. "Hey!" she cried. "What happened? I like my mittens."

"Oh, well," said Melody gaily. "Time to go inside."

Tulip stomped through the hallway to her classroom and plopped down at her desk. She pulled out a math worksheet. She had decorated the bottom with pictures of chickens wearing sneakers.

Melody leaned over for a closer look. "Did you draw those?" she asked.

"Yup," said Tulip proudly. "And it was really hard to get their beaks just right."

"But why are they wearing sneakers? I'd rather see their feet."

Just like that, the sneakers erased themselves from the page and were replaced with wrinkly chicken claws and spurs. "But—but—" sputtered Tulip.

"Much better," said Melody, and pulled out her own worksheet.

This was how Tulip's entire day went. Petulance Freeforall mentioned that she felt Tulip's jeans should be shorter, and—poof—they were shorter. "But I wanted them long!" cried Tulip.

"You're stepping on them. The bottoms are getting all frayed."

"That's *my* business."

Late that afternoon, Rusty stood in the doorway of his sister's room and said, "You know what? I think *your* room is too *neat*." Poof. Piles of clothes appeared on

Tulip's floor. Her bed unmade itself. Papers spilled off the desk, and dust bunnies floated into corners. A window shade fell down.

Rusty watched in satisfaction. "There. That's better."

"How is that better?" squawked Tulip.

"It looks like a normal bedroom."

"It does not!"

"I think it does."

"Well, that's just your opinion."

"And it's just *your* opinion," replied Rusty, "that Mom's earrings are too small and Dad's glasses are too round. Maybe they like them that way."

"Oh," said Tulip after a pause. She sat down on her rumpled bed in her too-short jeans. "And Mom did say she feels sad when the Christmas decorations come down." Suddenly Tulip put her hand to her mouth. "Oh no!"

"What?" asked Rusty, alarmed.

"I made Melody's hair short yesterday. I made her *braids* disappear. She must have felt awful."

Rusty pulled out his big sister's desk chair, shoved a heap of socks off it, and sat down. "You know," he said, feeling very wise, "if you realized that, like, I don't know, Dad was about to leave for work in his slippers, then you should say something to him. But you really don't need to mention every single dead fly. Or comment on people's habits."

"You're right," said Tulip.

In the hallway just outside, Helene and Marcel clutched hands and listened to their children holding a thoughtful, reasonable conversation.

"It's amazing," whispered Marcel.

"Maybe it's a dream," said Helene.

If they had peeked through the doorway at that moment, they would have seen Tulip's room tidy itself up, her jeans lengthen themselves, the gloves transform into mittens, and a line of chickens wearing sneakers march across a page of math problems.

On the other side of Little Spring Valley, Missy Piggle-Wiggle hummed a tune as she prepared supper.

8

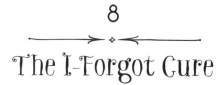

The I-Forgot Cure

IN MR. GARBER'S FIFTH-GRADE class at Little Spring Valley Elementary were eighteen desks—seventeen identical ones, and one with a footstool under it and a pillow on the chair. At the seventeen identical desks sat thirteen ten-year-olds and four eleven-year-olds. The desk with the footstool and the pillow belonged to Roseate Spoonbill, who had skipped two grades and was just eight years old. Without the pillow she could barely see over her desk, and without the footstool was left with her feet dangling in the air.

Rosie's mother had worried about skipping her so far ahead in school.

"The other students might be jealous of her big brain," said Selena Spoonbill to her husband, Vern. This was a year earlier, when she and Vern were driving home from Little Spring Valley Elementary, where they had just met with Rosie's second-grade teacher and the principal. "Skipping her all the way into fourth grade in the middle of the year? She'll be the only seven-year-old in a class of nine- and ten-year-olds. How will the older kids feel?"

"Feel about what?" said Vern.

"About a seven-year-old who can answer all the questions and is reading books the sixth graders are reading."

"Why, they'll feel impressed!" Rosie's father had replied cheerfully.

"I don't know," said Selena.

It turned out it didn't matter much that Rosie was seven and the rest of her classmates were older. After her first day in fourth grade, she'd come bouncing through the front door of her house and announced, "School was great! I told all my new friends that a roseate spoonbill is a wading bird found mostly in South

America, and they think I have a very cool name. One-third of them are going to call me Rosie, one-quarter of them are going to call me Roseate, and five-twelfths of them might call me Professor, but they aren't sure, and anyway, I like all the names so it doesn't matter."

"My goodness. Do you have any homework?" asked Selena. She worried that fourth-grade homework might be too much for Rosie, who still had a second-grade bedtime.

"Nope. I mean, I had homework, but I did it already."

"Are you sure? You didn't forget to do it, did you?"

Rosie sat down and thought. After a long time, she said, "No. I did it all after I finished my book during silent reading time."

"Okay," said her mother uncertainly.

Roseate Spoonbill, who was now in fifth grade, had many good qualities—but she was forgetful. She could remember anything she had ever read and anything she had ever learned about math or science or history, but most conversations with Rosie went something like this:

MRS. SPOONBILL: Time to go, Rosie. Your trumpet lesson is in half an hour.

ROSIE: *(after a very long pause)* What?

MRS. SPOONBILL: It's time to go.

ROSIE: Go where?

MRS. SPOONBILL: To your trumpet lesson. I just told you.

ROSIE: Oh. I forgot.

MRS. SPOONBILL: Did you remember to practice?

ROSIE: Practice?

MRS. SPOONBILL: Your *trumpet!*

ROSIE: Um, no, I guess I forgot that, too.

MRS. SPOONBILL: Well, come along. You can practice in the car.

ROSIE: All right. Just a minute.

Five minutes later:

MRS. SPOONBILL: Rosie? Are you ready?

ROSIE: Ready for what?

MRS. SPOONBILL: Your lesson. What *are* you doing?

ROSIE: Reading. Gosh, this is a good book.

Rosie's father fondly called her the absentminded professor. "Her brain is so jammed with facts and theories that it doesn't have any extra space for remembering things like practicing or brushing her teeth."

"But Dad," said Rosie's big brother, Montrose, "this morning she almost went to school wearing her pajama bottoms instead of pants. She is so embarrassing."

"Well, we caught her in time," said Vern.

Rosie's best friend was a girl named Poppy Fretwell, who was also in Mr. Garber's fifth-grade class. Poppy admired Rosie's big brain, but the truth was she was starting to find Rosie a lot of work. One day Poppy sat down in the cafeteria with her tray of food, and after a few minutes Rosie slid into the seat next to her.

"Where's your lunch?" asked Poppy.

"My lunch?"

"Yes. We're in the cafe*teria*? It's *lunch*time?"

"Oh. Yeah." Rosie looked at the empty table in front of her. "I guess I forgot my lunch."

"You can buy it, then."

"I guess I forgot to bring my money, too."

Poppy scrunched up her nose. A best friend, she knew, would offer her lunchless buddy some money so she could buy a sandwich. But Poppy had lent money to Rosie five times in the last month, and each time she had asked to be repaid, Rosie said, "Uh-oh. I forgot."

So Poppy gave Rosie half of her sandwich instead.

One night Mr. and Mrs. Spoonbill sat cozily in front of a fire after Roseate and Montrose had gone to bed. They were sipping tea, and Vern was scratching the ears of Honey, the cat who was curled in his lap. Suddenly his wife said, "We have to do something about Rosie. I know she's bright and she has deep thoughts in her head, but she forgets *every*thing, or she claims to. She doesn't feed Honey or practice her trumpet or take a bath without being told. She—"

"I know, I know. Our absentminded professor."

"But she needs to be responsible. She's eight and a half years old. When Montrose was her age, he was in charge of all the recycling. He did his chores without being asked. He even went to his piano lessons by himself."

"That's true. What do you propose?" asked Vern.

"Reminders," said his wife. "Simple reminders that can't be missed."

The next morning, when the Spoonbills gathered in

their kitchen for breakfast, Rosie saw a large sign taped to the refrigerator. It read:

FEED HONEY!!

But when Rosie and Montrose had scurried off to school, Selena felt Honey twining around her ankles, looked down, and saw that her dish was still empty. She asked Rosie about it that afternoon. "Oh, was that sign for me?" said Rosie.

"Yes, it was," her mother replied, and changed the sign to read:

ROSIE, FEED HONEY!!

But long after dinner that evening, Honey's dish was empty.

"Rosie, did you forget anything?" her mother asked her at bedtime.

"I probably forgot lots of things."

"What about Honey?"

"What about— Uh-oh. You know what happened? I took the sign into my room where I could see it, and then when I went back in the kitchen, there was no sign, so I forgot."

The next thing the Spoonbills tried was a chore chart for Rosie.

Montrose glared at it. "How come she gets a prize if she does her chores all week? That's no fair. I've been doing all my chores for years, and I don't get prizes."

"Don't worry. You'll also get a prize if you do your chores. It's just that you don't need a chart to keep track of things. You always remember."

Rosie was responsible for four chores each day. Since there are seven days in a week, there were twenty-eight boxes on her chart. At the end of the first week, two of them had been checked. The other twenty-six were blank.

"Ha-ha. Now you don't get a prize!" hooted Montrose.

"A prize?"

"*Yes!*" said her father. "That was the whole point of the chart. If you fill in all the boxes, you get a prize."

"Oh, yeah," said Rosie. "I forgot."

Montrose took the chart off the wall and tossed it in

the recycling bin, where he'd also put the reminder signs.

"I'm running out of ideas," Selena told her husband that night after Roseate had forgotten thirteen times in a single half hour to start taking her bath.

"We'll think of something."

Mr. and Mrs. Spoonbill sat down on the couch and rested their chins in their hands. They tapped their feet. Mr. Spoonbill scratched his head. They thought and thought. Finally his wife said, "I actually *am* out of ideas."

"So am I," her husband admitted.

"Sometimes I think Roseate 'forgets' on purpose."

"Really?"

"She only did two chores this week. That gave her plenty of time for lying around in her room."

"She doesn't lie around in her room. She studies! She reads articles. She thinks deep thoughts."

"And gets out of all her responsibilities."

"Hmm," said Vern Spoonbill.

The next morning as Rosie and Montrose were finishing breakfast, Mrs. Spoonbill said to her daughter, "Remember that you have soccer practice this afternoon. Go right to the field after school. Okay? *Right* to the *field*. No dawdling."

"And I'll go right to my piano lesson," said Montrose, just to prove that he didn't need reminders.

"Rosie?" said her mother. "What are you going to remember to do after school?"

"Huh?" said Rosie, who was thinking about penguins. Then she added, "Oh. Go to soccer practice."

〰〰〰

All that day Rosie's parents sat at their separate desks in their separate offices in their separate companies in a city not far from Little Spring Valley. Mr. Spoonbill was pleased that Rosie had remembered about soccer practice that morning. Perhaps, he thought, the reminder signs and the chore chart had had some effect after all.

Mrs. Spoonbill wasn't thinking about soccer. She had a big problem on her hands, a very boring grown-up thing involving money and investments. When her phone rang at 3:20, she picked it up without looking at the caller ID and said loudly, "I already told you to call Andi about this!"

There was a pause at the other end of the line, and

then she heard her husband say, "Call Andi about Rosie?"

"What?"

"What?"

"I'm sorry. I thought you were— Never mind. Is everything all right?"

"Rosie's coach just called. She isn't at practice."

Mrs. Spoonbill tried to stay calm. "She probably forgot and went home."

"I just called there. No one answered. But Poppy's at practice, and she said Rosie was in school all day. I guess I'd better run home and see what's going on."

Later, after all the excitement had died down, Montrose said that what happened that afternoon had felt like a TV show. "Rosie wasn't at practice, and she wasn't at home," he told Linden Pettigrew that night. "Mom and Dad called all her friends—the ones who aren't on the soccer team—and no one had seen her after school. That's when they called the police."

"Wow," Linden had replied, impressed. "The police!"

Nice Officer Belknap, one of only two officers in Little Spring Valley, had arrived at the Spoonbills' house in a hurry as soon as she got the call about a missing child. She sat in the living room across from Rosie's parents, who were side by side on the couch, wringing their hands. Montrose was sitting on the floor, Honey in his lap.

"We haven't seen her since she left for school this morning!" wailed Selena.

"But we know she was *in* school today," added Vern. "We just don't know where she went *after* school."

"We've called all her friends, and no one has seen her."

"Is she apt to wander off?" asked Officer Belknap. She was taking notes on her computer and looked up when the Spoonbills didn't answer right away.

"She's a bit forgetful," Selena said finally.

"A *bit* forgetful?!" exclaimed Montrose.

"Aren't you going to start doing something?" Vern asked the officer. "She's been missing for two hours."

"Who's been missing for two hours?" asked a voice from the doorway.

Mr. and Mrs. Spoonbill leaped to their feet.

"Rosie!" cried her mother.

"Where have you *been?*" asked her father.

Selena and Vern pulled their daughter to them in a tight hug.

"I was at school. In the library. I guess I lost track of the time. All of a sudden the custodian was turning out the lights, and I realized I should leave. How come Officer Belknap is here?"

"Because you didn't go to soccer practice and nobody knew where you were! We didn't know *what* had happened," exclaimed Mrs. Spoonbill. "We were so worried!"

"Oh, yeah. Soccer practice," said Roseate, and slapped herself on the head. "I guess I forgot. I found this great book about penguins."

"But we gave you reminders," said her mother, just as her father said, "This has got to stop. We called the *police*, Rosie. What happened today is serious. Do you understand that?"

"Am I in trouble?" asked Roseate in a small voice.

"Well, we certainly have to figure out what to do about this."

Officer Belknap got to her feet. "If everything is okay here, I'll be going."

"Thank you so much for your help," said Rosie's mother.

~~~~~~

That night at dinner Rosie looked around at her family and said, "You know what you should do? You should call Missy Piggle-Wiggle about me."

"Who's Missy Piggle-Wiggle?" asked Selena.

"She's the lady who lives in that upside-down house that's right side up," replied Montrose. "With the pig and the parrot."

"She cures children," added Rosie. "Whenever any of my friends are having trouble, their parents phone Missy."

"I don't know," said Vern, looking across the table at his wife and wrinkling his nose. "An upside-down house? A pig and a parrot?"

"Poppy was suffering from Candyitis," said Rosie, "and Missy cured her."

"But just so you know, Missy's house is under quarantine," added Montrose. He lowered his voice and whispered, "The Effluvia."

Selena was about to say that there must be a better way to cure Rosie when she remembered the sight of Officer Belknap's patrol car in the driveway that afternoon. "Why don't we give Missy a try?" she said to her husband.

~~~~~

The Spoonbills called Missy later that night when Rosie and Montrose were busy with their homework. Selena expected a dry, creaky old voice to answer the phone, but the voice on the other end of the line sounded light and bubbly.

"Is this Missy Piggle-Wiggle?" asked Vern.

"It is. And you're Rosie's parents? She's a lovely girl."

"You know Rosie?" asked Selena.

"Of course. She's been here many times. I expect she forgot to tell you."

"Well, yes," agreed the Spoonbills.

"That's why we're calling," added Vern.

In the kitchen of the right-side-up upside-down house, Missy nodded her head, her springy hair bouncing around her face. "I'll package up the Forget-fulness Cure tonight, and you can pick it up tomor-row."

"I heard that your house is under quarantine," said Selena.

"Yes, but probably not for too much longer," Missy replied as Lightfoot floated into the room. She was sev-eral feet lower than usual and came to a neat stop on the kitchen table. "I'll leave the bag on the front porch. You won't catch anything. Now, just follow the instruc-tions. I'll call you at the end of the week to find out how things are going."

Missy clicked off the phone and watched as Penel-ope swooped through the doorway and landed on the counter. "How about a snack?" she squawked, and flapped her wings. "How about a snack?"

Missy smiled and opened the container of parrot food. She let out a small sigh of relief. "I'm glad you're feeling better," she said.

At six o'clock the next evening, Roseate's parents sat in their living room, huddled over the bag Vern had picked up at Missy's house. Selena began to open it gingerly.

"I don't think anything is going to spring out," said her husband.

"Really? From a bag picked up at a formerly upside-down house where a magical woman named Piggle-Wiggle lives with a parrot and a pig?"

"Hmm," said Vern. He set the bag on the coffee table and found a yardstick. Then he and Selena backed away as he carefully opened the bag with the end of the stick.

Nothing happened.

The Spoonbills crept closer. At last Selena worked up the courage to peer inside the bag. "The only thing in there is a peppermint candy," she reported.

"Seriously? A piece of candy?"

"Well, and a note that says to give this to Rosie after dinner tonight."

"Does the note say what the candy will do?"

"Nope."

"What do you think?"

At that moment Rosie ambled into the living room and said, "I forgot to bring my books home from school.

Can somebody drive me over there? I can't do my homework without my books."

"I think," Mrs. Spoonbill said to her husband, "that Rosie is going to have a peppermint for dessert tonight."

~~~~~

That evening Rosie sat in the kitchen with her parents and licked the last of the peppermint off her fingers. "How come you're staring at me?" she said. "You've been staring at me for forty-six seconds."

"Have we?" said her father.

Rosie nodded. "Why?"

Mr. and Mrs. Spoonbill glanced at each other. "That's funny," said Vern. "I forget."

"You forget why you've been staring at me?"

"Yes," said her father.

"We were staring?" said her mother.

Rosie shrugged and went upstairs to her room. She lay on her bed and opened her science book. The first thing she saw was a picture of a penguin, so she closed the book, opened her laptop, and searched for information on Antarctica.

Two hours passed. Rosie sat up suddenly. The clock

on her computer read 10:09. Rosie had a feeling that by 10:09, her parents had usually told her to go to bed. She stuck her head into the hallway. Montrose's light was on in his room. She could hear the TV downstairs.

"Montrose?" she said. "Are you still up?"

"I'm reading."

"Aren't we supposed to be in bed?"

"Gosh, I guess so."

Rosie ran downstairs. "Mom? Dad? How come you didn't tell me to go to bed?"

"To go to bed?" said her father.

"What time is it?" asked her mother.

"It's after ten."

"I guess we forgot," said Mr. Spoonbill.

Her parents stood up and wandered out of the room.

"You didn't turn off the TV," Rosie called after them.

"Oh dear. We forgot," said Mrs. Spoonbill.

Frowning, Rosie turned off the TV and then all the lights before following her parents upstairs. She put herself to bed that night feeling very puzzled.

The next morning when Rosie awoke, she lay in her deliciously warm bed and thought how pleasant it was not to be disturbed by anyone knocking at her door and telling her to get up. After a while she noticed bright sun shining around the edges of her blinds. She peeked outside and saw a school bus disappearing down the street. Rosie's eyes widened. She looked at her computer. Eight o'clock.

"Hey! Hey, everybody! It's eight o'clock!" Rosie squawked, sounding quite a bit like Penelope. She heaved herself out of bed and threw open her door. The house was silent. Her parents were asleep in their room. Montrose was asleep in his room. "Get up! Get up! We're going to be late! The school bus has already left."

"What?" murmured her parents.

"Didn't you set your alarm?" asked Rosie.

"Huh. I guess we forgot," her father mumbled.

"Well, come on! We're going to be late for school!" squealed Rosie. "And I don't want to be late. I haven't been marked late once, and I want a perfect record."

There was a lot of scurrying around then. Closets were flung open and toilets were flushed. When the

Spoonbills finally ran into the kitchen, Rosie cried, "Mom, you're still in your pajamas!"

"Oops. I forgot to get dressed!"

"And, uh-oh, I forgot to make your lunches," said her father.

"Mom, you get dressed. I'll make some sandwiches," said Rosie. "Goodness, I have to do everything around here." She slapped together two bologna sandwiches, fed Honey, and handed her father the car keys. "If you drive us, we won't be late," she told him. "Mom, remember to put on *all* your clothes! Shoes, too." She clapped her hands. "Let's go, let's go, let's go!"

Ten minutes later Rosie slid into her seat in Mr. Garber's room. She was just in time to shout "Here!" when he called her name.

~~~~~

That evening the Spoonbills gathered around their dining room table. Rosie sniffed the air. "What's for dinner?" she asked.

"Hamburgers?" suggested Montrose hopefully.

"Did you pick up something at the Snack Shoppe?" asked Rosie.

"Uh-oh. We forgot," said Mr. Spoonbill.

"Forgot about dinner?" said Rosie.

"Well, yes."

Rosie sniffed the air again. "Did you forget anything else?" she asked.

"Such as?" said her mother.

"Well," said Rosie, "I took a bath this afternoon, but when was the last time any of you took a shower?"

"Hmm," said Montrose.

"Um," said her mother.

"There wasn't enough time this morning," said her father. "We overslept."

"That's because you forgot to set your alarm!" exclaimed Rosie, exasperated. "Now listen to me. Enough is enough. The three of you march upstairs and take showers. I'll make something for dinner. Go!"

Rosie opened cupboard doors. She pawed through the refrigerator. Finally she yelled upstairs, "Did anyone remember to go to the grocery store today?"

"I guess I forgot," her mother called back.

"I don't hear the water running," Rosie continued. "Are you guys taking your showers?"

"Showers?" replied Mr. Spoonbill, Mrs. Spoonbill, and Montrose.

Rosie abandoned the kitchen and stomped up the stairs. She turned on the shower in her parents' bathroom. "One of you go in there right now. And use soap!" Then she turned on the shower in the bathroom she and Montrose shared. She handed her brother a washcloth. "I expect you to be clean when you come downstairs."

Rosie returned to the kitchen and decided that the only thing she could make for dinner was leftovers. *I'll call it potluck*, she thought. *That sounds better.* She was setting out the last of the mysterious little containers she had found in the refrigerator when she realized she could still hear the water running upstairs.

"Is someone still showering?" she called.

"What?" said her brother.

"Showering?" said her father.

"Oh dear," said her mother.

Rosie plunked down on the floor at the bottom of the stairs. She felt like crying. But a thought was buzzing around in her brain like a fly, so instead she stood up and shouted, "Could you all come down here, please? We need to have a talk."

"Right now?" asked her father.

"Yes. Right. Now. Oh, but turn off the water first."

When the four Spoonbills were seated in the living room, Rosie said, "Something has to change around here. I cannot be responsible for all of you. Do you understand? We have to *share* responsibilities. That's how families work. So starting right now we will follow the to-do lists I'm about to make, and we will check off our chores on the chart I'm about to make. Is that understood?"

"I suppose," said Mr. Spoonbill.

"But why is it so important?" asked Mrs. Spoonbill.

"Because otherwise things kind of fall apart," said Rosie. Suddenly she remembered the look on her parents' faces when she'd returned home and found them talking to Officer Belknap. She remembered all the times she'd asked them to bring her forgotten homework to school, all the times she'd borrowed lunch money from Poppy, forgotten to practice her trumpet or feed Honey or take a bath. "I'm sorry," she added, looking first at her parents and then at

Montrose. "Really sorry. Things are going to change. You'll see."

Rosie worked hard that evening and managed to make the lists and charts *and* finish her homework and still go to bed on time.

By the end of the week, the Spoonbill household was nicely organized.

"Maybe we don't need prizes for completing our chores," said Mr. Spoonbill on Friday evening.

"Okay," said Rosie, who was relieved, since she didn't have enough money to buy prizes for everyone.

"I don't think we even need the charts and lists," added Mrs. Spoonbill.

"Maybe not. You guys seem to remember everything now anyway. But I kind of like the charts and lists. Let's leave them up for a while."

On Sunday evening at eight o'clock on the dot, Mrs. Spoonbill's phone rang. "It's Missy Piggle-Wiggle," she said to her husband.

"How are things going?" asked Missy.

"Perfectly!" exclaimed Roseate's parents.

"Do you need another peppermint?"

"No!"

"Absolutely not!"

Then Mrs. Spoonbill added, "Thank you, Missy. You've worked wonders."

At the right-side-up upside-down house, Missy clicked off her phone. She bent to stroke Lightfoot, who was walking casually across the parlor floor. Then she turned to Penelope and announced, "All cured." Penelope replied, "I knew it!"

And then Missy looked at poor Lester, who was lying on the couch with a cold cloth on his cheek. "Hmm," she said. "Hmm."

9

Melody Saves the Day

VERY EARLY ONE morning—in the darkest hours after midnight—Missy Piggle-Wiggle was awakened by a great rumbling and jumbling. Most people would have thought they were in the middle of an earthquake, but Missy sat up in bed and said to Lightfoot, who was snoozing next to her, "Ah. I expect House is back to rights." She turned on the light. Sprouting out of her bedroom floor was the chandelier. The doorway was once again upside down. The window was upside down. "Perfect," said Missy. "House is over the flu. So are you," she added, patting Lightfoot. "And you," she said to Penelope, who was perched on the end of the bed.

Then Missy sneezed. She sneezed again. She reached for a tissue and blew her nose.

"Pipe down!" squawked Penelope.

"I cad't help it," said Missy stuffily. "I dod't feel well. I thick I have the flu."

"Just a cold!" said Penelope.

"Baybe. But it feels like bore thad a cold."

Missy fell asleep again. She tossed and turned. When she awoke in the morning, she stretched and discovered that her entire body ached. "Evedd by hair hurts," she complained to Wag, who had joined her on the bed.

"Impossible!" screeched Penelope.

"Doe, really. By hair hurts. By head hurts." She gulped in some air and sneezed five times. "Add why is the heat od so high?" She put a hand to her forehead. "Oh. I guess it isd't. I have a fever."

"Breakfast time!" said Penelope, bouncing up and down.

"Ugh," said Missy, but she rolled out of bed and fed

Wag, Lightfoot, Lester, and Penelope. Then she phoned Harold. "I have the flu," she told him.

"The Winter Effluvia?"

"Baybe. I hate to ask this, but could you cub over add feed the adibals id the bard?"

"What?"

"The adibals id the bard. You doe, Trotsky, Bartha and Billard Ballard . . ."

"Oh, the animals in the barn!" said Harold. "Yes, of course."

"Dod't cub id the house," croaked Missy, and coughed. "Everythig you deed is id the bard. The house is still quaradteed. Oh, but House is over the flu, so it's upside dowd agaid."

"Okay," said Harold. "Don't worry. I'll take care of everything. I'm going to leave some chicken soup on your porch. Get lots of rest and call if you need anything else." He paused. "I miss you."

"I biss you, too."

Missy lay on the couch in the parlor and covered herself with a blanket. As everyone knows, there's nothing dogs and cats like better than a sick person, and in a matter of minutes, Missy was joined by Wag and Lightfoot, who were hot but comforting. Lester sat across from her in an armchair, and Penelope perched behind him. The five of them dozed and dreamed until the phone rang late in the afternoon.

Missy reached for it. "Hello?" she croaked.

"Is this . . . Penelope?"

"Doe, it's Bissy."

"Missy? This is Melody. You don't sound like yourself. What's wrong with your voice?"

"The flu," said Missy sadly.

There was a very long pause before Melody said, "Oh. I walked by your house after school and saw that it's upside down again. But the quarantine signs are still posted. Now I know why." She sighed. She felt a little like crying because it had been such a long time since she'd seen her friend, but an idea was starting to come to her, so she straightened up and said, "Missy, I'm going to call you back later if that's okay." Then she clicked off her phone and stretched out on her bed.

Melody thought about what a good friend Missy was to the children of Little Spring Valley. She thought how disappointed she was every time she passed the upside-down house and saw the quarantine signs.

"They've been up *forever!*" she'd cried to Tulip one day, which of course was not true, but that was how long it felt.

I wish, Melody thought now as she folded her arms behind her head, *that I could help Missy. She's always helping my friends and me. If I were a good friend, I would help her.* Melody tossed ideas around for fifteen more minutes before she picked up her phone again. "Missy," she said, "I think I have a cure for you. Well, no, that's not quite true. I think I know *where* to find a cure for you, for the Effluvia."

"You do?" replied Missy. She propped herself up on one elbow. "A cure for the Effluvia?"

"Yes. I'm going to go to the Art of Magic."

"The bagic store? It's dot eved opedd, is it?"

"It is open. It's open all year long now. And you're always curing my friends with magic, so maybe I can cure you with magic. I really want to! I'm going to buy something at the store."

"Belody," said Missy gently, "that's a lovely thought. Thack you. But rebebber that the store odly sells tricks add costubes add props. Thigs like that. Dot adythig to do with real bagic."

"There must be *some*thing at the store. Something that's real magic. Remember Snowman the cat?"

Missy sat up even farther. Her breath caught in her throat. Finally she managed to croak, "Sdowbad. I wodder."

That was all Melody needed to hear. "Don't worry, Missy. I have a plan." (This was close to the truth.) Melody suddenly felt very grown-up. "Now, leave everything to me. You just rest and get plenty of sleep. And drink lots of fluids. Juice and tea and stuff. I'm going to take care of the flu once and for all."

~~~~~~

As school drew to an end the next afternoon, Melody felt butterflies flapping around in her stomach. So she had a little talk with herself. *You can do this. You've been to the Art of Magic before.* (Just not without Missy.) *And you want to help your friend. You can do this,* she thought again. *You CAN do this. Be brave.*

Melody took a different route home from school that day. She pointed her feet sternly in the direction of Juniper Street. "Go," she told them. She reached Juniper, crossed it, walked to Spell Street, and passed by all

the nice, regular shops there, coming to a halt when she reached the sign with the black top hat and the red wand over the words THE ART OF MAGIC. The sign swayed a bit even though Melody couldn't detect a breeze. She looked at the crumbling cement steps leading into darkness. Then she marched down those steps to the door below and, before she could think too much about what she was doing, twisted the knob and thrust herself inside the darkened room.

She braced for what was coming.

"Welcome to your doom," intoned a tinny voice.

Melody squeezed her eyes shut. *It isn't real. It isn't a person. It's just like the sneezing door at Harold's bookstore.*

"Hello!" called Art Magic from behind the counter. Then he added cheerfully, "Mwa-ha-ha! What can I do for you?"

Melody listened to her pounding heart and whispered, "I was wondering if you have any cures for the Winter Effluvia."

Art frowned. "What?"

"That's okay. I'll just look around."

"Well, let me know if you need any help." Art was wearing a black robe with a brilliant scarlet lining. The robe reminded Melody of a bird she'd once seen—a bird whose red feathers had appeared when it had spread its tail and sailed off a tree branch, then had disappeared when it came to rest again. On Art's head was a witch's hat that kept sliding down over his eyebrows; finally it slipped off completely, landing in a container of takeout food from the Snack Shoppe.

"Snakes and snails," Art muttered, reaching for a roll of paper towels.

Melody's heart stopped pounding, and she put her hand over her mouth so she wouldn't giggle. Feeling much braver, she wound her way along the aisles, pretending to examine the tricks and costumes and decks of cards. At last she saw what she was looking for.

"Snowman!" she said in a loud whisper. "There you are."

The black cat was sleeping on a low shelf, where he had wedged himself between a box labeled LEVITATION TRICKS and a box labeled COIN EFFECTS.

Melody put out a hand and stroked his head. "You don't look very comfortable," she told him.

Snowman opened one golden eye and began to purr. Then he closed the eye.

"I need to have a talk with you," said Melody. "I know you can hear me, and I know you can understand me." She glanced down the aisle to make sure Art was still busy behind the counter. "It's about the flu," she continued. "And not the regular flu, the Winter Effluvia." Snowman opened both of his eyes. "Everyone at the upside-down house caught it. Well, almost everyone. And I really, really, really want to help Missy get well. You remember Missy. So . . . could you cast a spell? Or something?"

Snowman sat up and his eyes blazed.

"Does that mean yes?" asked Melody.

Snowman blinked.

Melody cocked her head. "It does. I know it does." She patted Snowman once more, then stood and walked back to the counter.

"Find what you were looking for?" asked Art.

"Sort of. Mr. Magic, I was wondering if, um, I could borrow Snowman for a few days. I have an important mission for him."

Now, in most cases, if a stranger asked if she could borrow someone's cat, the answer, of course, would be no—unless the stranger she was talking to was named

Art Magic and the conversation was taking place in the town of Little Spring Valley.

"An important mission?" asked Art. "How important?"

"Very important," Melody replied solemnly.

Art sat silently behind the counter for a few moments. Then he pushed the witch's hat back up on his head, tapped a finger on his nose, and let out a "Hmm."

Melody's heart began to pound again.

At last Art said, "Just let me pack his suitcase."

"He has a suitcase?"

"Of course."

Art disappeared through a door at the back of the store. Melody leaned around a display of wands and said to Snowman, "He's packing your suitcase."

Snowman got to his feet and trotted toward Melody. Presently Art came back through the door carrying a small blue bag. "Everything Snowman needs is in here," he said. "Food and so forth. His blankie."

Snowman puffed up his tail, and Art said, "He's embarrassed about the blankie." Then he leaned toward Melody and whispered, "But he needs it at night."

"Thank you, Mr. Magic," Melody said politely. She reached for the suitcase. "Where's his carrier?"

"His carrier? Oh, he doesn't have one. He'll just walk along beside you."

"On a leash?"

"Nope. You'll see."

Melody started for the door to the stairs, and Art stooped down to give Snowman a pat. "Be a good boy. And be helpful. I'll see you soon."

"Mroww," said Snowman, and bounded across the shop to catch up with Melody. They climbed the stairs, the words "Welcome to your doom" fading behind them.

Melody looked down at the little cat as they started along Spell Street. "Thank you so much for helping out, Snowman. I hope you don't mind being away from home. Missy Piggle-Wiggle really needs you. You and your magic. This is very important."

Snowman glanced at Melody, then resumed his graceful walk, delicately stepping around puddles and mounds of dirty snow. If anyone thought the sight of a girl and a cat hurrying through town together was unusual, they didn't say so.

After several blocks Melody turned off Juniper Street and onto the road to Missy's. A few minutes later she said, "Here we are, Snowman."

Snowman plunked his hindquarters down on the end of the path through the yard and stared.

"I know. The house is upside down," said Melody.

Snowman blinked, got to his feet again, and ran ahead of Melody to Missy's front door. Melody could hear Penelope screech, "Missy, Melody and some cat are here!"

Snowman turned blazing eyes to Melody.

"I'm sorry Penelope called you 'some cat,'" she said hastily. "You just have to get used to her." Melody bent down and peered through the window on the door that was now nicely upside down again.

"Belody? Is that you?" Missy's face appeared on the other side of the window.

"I brought you help. Magic help! I told you I would." Melody picked up Snowman and held him so that his face was just inches from Missy's. "Snowman's going to cure you and get rid of the flu. Forever," she added, even though she had absolutely no idea what Snowman was capable of.

"Belody," Missy started to say.

"No, really. I want to help. Mr. Magic said it was okay for Snowman to stay here for a while. He packed his suitcase and everything." Melody set Snowman down and held up the bag.

"Well . . . thack you," croaked Missy. "I appreciate this. You're a good fred, Belody."

Melody grinned. Then she ran along the path to the street and turned around in time to watch Missy open her front door and usher Snowman inside.

~~~~~

Melody had intended to wait until after school the next day before calling to find out how things were going at the upside-down house, but at seven o'clock in the morning, she found herself punching in Missy's phone number. She expected to hear a croaking, coughing voice say, "Hello?"

Instead she heard a perky, "Good morning, Melody!"

"Missy? Is that really you? You sound like yourself again."

"It's really me, and I feel much better."

"What kind of magic did Snowman do?"

There was a pause at Missy's end of the line before she said, "I don't know. Mostly he sat around and blinked. And tried to ignore Lightfoot when she swatted him."

"That's strange." Melody had expected to hear that Snowman had set candles aflame by staring at them or had sent objects flying through the air, even though she didn't know how those things might have helped Missy. She let out a sigh. Then she said, "Lightfoot swatted at Snowman?"

"Yes, she was quite rude. I think she's jealous of him."

"So Snowman didn't do *anything*? I mean, anything magic?"

"Not that I saw. Of course I don't know what he did at night while I was asleep."

"At night!" exclaimed Melody. "That must have been when he worked his magic. Probably on the dot of midnight."

"I suppose. . . ." said Missy.

"I'm going to stop by after school to see how you're doing."

~~~~~~

Melody kept her promise, but she wasn't Missy's first visitor that day. Shortly before lunchtime, when Missy realized that she truly felt as right as rain again, she phoned Harold.

"So the flu is gone?" he cried. "Everyone is well? Even Lester?"

"Lester isn't himself, but I don't think he has the flu after all." She lowered her voice. "I think he misses my great-aunt."

"Oh dear," murmured Harold. Then he added that he would be over in a flash. By the time he arrived, Missy had taken the quarantine signs down.

"Missy!" Harold exclaimed.

"Harold!"

The door to the upside-down house was wide open, but Harold stood on the porch, shuffling his feet and holding his hands behind his back.

"What are you waiting for?" screeched Penelope. "Come inside."

Harold stepped into the hallway and produced a

bouquet of spring flowers for Missy. "I—I—" he stammered.

"Spit it out!" called Penelope. "Say whatever it is you want to say."

Missy turned around and shushed the parrot. Then she turned back to Harold. "I didn't know I was going to miss you so much."

"I didn't know *I* would miss *you* so much."

"Come, let's have some tea."

In the kitchen, Missy filled the kettle and found a vase for the flowers. Then she sat next to Harold and took his hands in hers.

When school ended at Little Spring Valley Elementary that day, Melody ran through the front door, across the yard to the sidewalk, and all the way through town to the upside-down house. The first thing she noticed was that the signs were gone. She let out a whoop. She had a feeling that she should turn right around and tell her friends they could visit Missy again, but she didn't want one more second to go by before she saw Missy herself.

She ran to the porch and skidded to a stop just as, from inside, Penelope called, "Melody's here!"

When the door opened, Melody leaped forward and gave Missy a fierce hug. "Is the Winter Effluvia really gone?"

"It's really gone."

Melody let another whoop. She called hello to Lightfoot, to Wag, to Penelope, and to Snowman, who was sitting placidly on the bottom step of the staircase, his tail wrapped neatly around his front legs. Then she caught sight of Lester reclining on the couch in the parlor. "Hello, Lester!"

Lester waved one front hoof. Then he held the hoof to his cheek.

"Oh," said Melody. "Does Lester have a toothache?"

Missy opened her mouth. She closed it. She stared at Lester. "*Do* you have a toothache?"

Lester's eyes filled with tears. He nodded.

"All this time? You've had a toothache?" said Missy. She sat next to Lester and patted his back. "Why didn't you let me know?"

Lester shrugged.

"I'll bet I know why," spoke up Melody. "He doesn't want to go to the dentist."

Lester hung his head, but Missy said, "Don't worry. We'll get it taken care of, and you'll feel much better."

Fifteen minutes later Melody called good-bye to Missy and left the upside-down house with Snowman and his suitcase. As she walked him back to the Art of Magic, she passed her friends on their way home from school and said to each one, "The flu is gone! We can visit Missy again!"

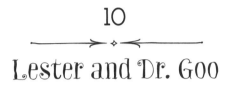

10

Lester and Dr. Goo

BY THE TIME Melody had returned Snowman to Art Magic, said her thank-yous, and rushed back to Missy's, she found children teeming through the upside-down house, running from room to room, outside to the barn, and around to the front yard, where the earliest spring flowers were just beginning to poke through the earth. Rusty Goodenough and Roseate Spoonbill were building a fort under the dining room table. Einstein Treadupon was reading a magazine to Wag. Children were knitting and cooking and arguing and laughing.

Melody found Missy helping Veronica Cupcake

fashion parrot clothes for Penelope. "Did you make an appointment for Lester?" she asked.

"I did," Missy replied. "He's going to see Dr. Goo tomorrow afternoon."

Melody had never heard of Dr. Goo, but since she didn't have a pet, she didn't know the vets in town. "Can I go with you? I could help you keep Lester calm."

"Of course," said Missy. "We'll meet you at your house at three thirty tomorrow."

~~~~~

The next afternoon Missy walked to Melody's house, holding Lester by one front hoof. He moved slowly, scuffing his hind feet along the sidewalk.

"I know you don't want to go," said Missy patiently, "but Dr. Goo is going to make you feel better."

Lester walked even more slowly.

"Please come along. If we don't walk faster, we're going to be late."

Lester slowed to a crawl.

"Luckily Dr. Goo said he'll see you today no matter what, so you might as well hurry up. Anyway, you haven't been outside in ages. Doesn't it feel good to be outdoors? Doesn't the sun feel nice on your face? You can smell springtime in the air."

Lester shrugged.

"Missy! Lester!"

Ahead, Missy caught sight of Melody running through her yard. Melody opened the gate in the fence and came running. "Hi, Lester. Are you ready for Dr. Goo?"

Lester turned his face away.

"You don't have to be scared," said Melody. "My dentist is really nice, so I'll bet Dr. Goo is, too. I always get a prize when I leave. The last time I got a yo-yo."

Lester narrowed his eyes and held out his hoofs.

"Well, I know you can't work a yo-yo, but Dr. Goo probably has plenty of other prizes. I'm sure you'll get a nice treat."

Lester glared at her.

"I'm afraid Lester isn't in a mood to be cheered up," Missy told Melody. "Don't worry. I know he's glad you're here."

Melody took Lester by his other front hoof and the three of them set off, hand in hoof, for Juniper Street. When they reached it, they turned left instead of right. Lester came to a halt and tilted his head at Missy.

"This is the right way," she told him. "Dr. Goo's office is at the very edge of town."

Lester nodded, and the three of them set off again. They walked past stores and houses and a big grocery store. They walked until the road began to narrow and eventually became a wide path through thick woods.

"Is this *really* the way to Dr. Goo's?" asked Melody. "It's kind of dark in here."

"Look ahead," replied Missy, pointing.

Melody squinted. "Oh!" In the distance was a stone building with an oaken door and ivy climbing the walls. "It looks like a cottage in a fairy tale," she said.

Above the door was a sign shaped like an enormous tooth. On the tooth were the words DR. GOO.

Lester saw the tooth and sat down on the path.

"Lester," said Missy. "Come along."

Lester shook his head.

"We can sit here as long as you want, but eventually Dr. Goo will come outside and look in your mouth right here."

Lester sighed loudly and stood up.

Missy opened the door under the tooth, and she and Melody and Lester stepped inside. A man and a woman were sitting behind the reception desk. In the waiting room were a gray-haired man, a young woman, and a small boy.

Everyone screamed when they saw Lester, and the gray-haired man spilled his coffee.

"Missy!" cried Melody. "What kind of office is this?"

"It's a dentist's office."

"I know, but is Dr. Goo a dentist for animals or for people?"

"Well . . . I don't know. I just made an appointment with a dentist."

The woman behind the desk gulped in some air. She fanned her face. Then she said, "Everyone is welcome here." She drew in another deep breath. "You must be Lester Piggle-Wiggle," she added.

Lester nodded. He was holding his hoof to his cheek again.

"Dr. Goo will see you in about twenty minutes. And don't worry. He'll have you feeling fine in no time. Please have a seat."

Lester edged into the waiting room. He took a seat by the woman. Missy and Melody sat across from him.

The room grew absolutely silent. No one moved. No one spoke.

After a while, Lester reached for a magazine, and the boy turned to his mother and said, "Mommy, can that pig read?"

The woman watched Lester turn pages. "I suppose so," she said weakly.

A young girl came out of Dr. Goo's office then. She ran to the woman, holding a prize above her head. "Mom! Look what I got! It's a—" She saw Lester, dropped the prize, and shrieked.

"Come along, darling," said her mother, and she hustled the children out the door.

Presently, the man who had spilled his coffee was ushered back to Dr. Goo's office. At last Missy, Melody, and Lester were the only ones in the waiting room.

"Lester," said Melody, "are you smiling?"

Lester pretended to scream and knock over a cup of coffee, and Melody began to laugh.

Lester grinned. But when the door to the waiting room opened and a dental assistant called, "Lester Piggle-Wiggle?" Lester's smile faded. Slowly he stood up.

The woman turned pale. "You're Lester?"

He nodded.

"But you're a pig."

"That's as may be," spoke up Missy, "but he still needs to have his tooth taken care of."

"Come with me, then," said the woman, glancing around the waiting room as if she might find some other pigs there. "My name is Sarah."

Lester turned to look at Missy and Melody.

"May we come in, too?" asked Melody. "Lester needs us."

Several minutes later Lester was settled in a chair in an examining room. Missy and Melody stood by the window. They waited quietly until the door opened, and in walked a pleasant-looking young man who was trying very hard to smile.

"Hello, everyone," he said. "I'm Dr. Goo. I understand we have a porcine patient here."

"A what?" asked Melody.

"Well, a pig."

"A pig with a toothache," Missy told him. "It's been bothering him for quite some time now."

"I must confess that I've never worked on a pig," said Dr. Goo.

"Oh, it shouldn't be too difficult," Missy told him cheerfully. "Teeth are teeth. Open wide, Lester."

Lester opened his mouth and bared his teeth.

"My!" exclaimed Dr. Goo. "They certainly are large. Those canines look more like, well, fangs."

Lester snapped his mouth shut, offended.

"I believe they're called tusks," said Missy. "Open up again, Lester."

Dr. Goo shone a bright light in Lester's mouth and peered inside. "Mm-hmm, mm-hmm."

"What do you see?" asked Missy.

Dr. Goo frowned. Lester's eyes grew wide. Melody leaned over and patted his arm. "It's okay," she whispered.

"Well," said Dr. Goo after a moment, "I see a lot of brown teeth."

"Lester, have you been brushing?" Missy asked.

Lester pretended not to hear her.

"Lester?"

He shook his head.

"Can you point to the tooth that's bothering you?" Dr. Goo asked.

Lester indicated a tooth far in the back, on the left side.

"This one?"

Lester nodded.

Dr. Goo leaned in for an even closer look. "Mm-hmm, mm-hmm," he murmured again. "You have a cavity, all right. But we'll get it filled, and you'll be feeling better in no time. Now," he went on as he began to assemble instruments on his tray, "I'd like to talk to you about brushing your teeth."

"That sounds like a good idea," said Missy.

"What kind of toothbrush do you use?" asked Dr. Goo. "Do you have a nice big one for those choppers?"

"He has a regular brush," said Missy, "but I doubt he's been using it."

"We'll see if we can't find you a proper-sized brush. Okay, Lester. Here we go."

Missy and Melody held tight to Lester's hoof.

~~~~~

When Dr. Goo straightened up later and said, "All done. That wasn't so bad, was it?" Lester looked at the dentist in surprise. He even gave him a lopsided smile.

"You were very brave," said Melody.

"Thank you," replied Dr. Goo. "As I said, I've never worked on a pig before."

"I meant that Lester was brave. But you were brave, too," said Melody kindly.

"Lester, you were extra brave," agreed Missy. "And very patient. Now, if you'll just remember to brush your teeth every day, you can avoid cavities."

"And look what Sarah found while I was filling your tooth." Dr. Goo handed Lester an enormous brush. "It should reach all your teeth easily. Take especially good care of those fa—uh, those tusks."

"Does he get a prize?" asked Melody.

"He certainly does." Now Dr. Goo produced a tube of toothpaste. "It's coffee-flavored," he said, and Lester's eyes brightened.

"How did you know he likes coffee?" asked Melody.

"Just a hunch. Okay, Lester, you're all set to go."

Missy, Melody, and Lester walked along Juniper Street until they were back in town. Then they kept going until they were standing outside A to Z Books. Missy waved through the window to Harold, and he waved back. A moment later he switched off the lights in the store, turned the sign on the door so that it read CLOSED, stepped outside, and locked the door.

"All better?" he said to Lester.

Lester held up his new toothbrush and the tube of coffee toothpaste and offered Harold a smile. Then Harold took Missy by the hand, and Melody took Lester by the hoof, and the four of them set off for the upside-down house.

That night, when the animals had been settled into the barn, and Lester was tucked into his bed, Missy sat at the table in her warm kitchen. Wag and Lightfoot curled up on the floor next to her. She chewed thoughtfully on the end of a pen and wrote *Dear Auntie*. Then she set the pen down. "Where to begin?" she said aloud. Wag glanced at her sleepily. Missy thought about the Effluvia. She thought about Lester's tooth. She thought about the right-side-up house and the Sticky-Fingers Cure and the Pants-on-Fire Cure. There was so much news, Missy thought it could fill a book.

Finally she picked up the pen again and wrote: *Things here at the upside-down house are fine.* She crossed out *fine* and wrote *never dull.* She crossed out *never dull* and decided to start over with a fresh piece of paper.

Missy didn't know where Mrs. Piggle-Wiggle was, or

Dear Auntie,

Greetings from Little Spring Valley. In your last letter you asked a very important question. You asked if I could carry on at the upside-down house. Here is my answer: YES!

I love Lester and Wag and Lightfoot and Penelope. I love the barn animals. I love the children in town. I love spending time with Harold Spectacle. Every day I'm learning new things about cures and potions.

How wonderful that you and Uncle are together again, and that you're sailing the world. Sail and explore for as long as you want. The upside-down house is safe, and I am happy—very, very happy—to stay here for as long as I'm needed.

Your loving and devoted niece Missy

where she might be in a week or two weeks or a month. But she knew just how to send the letter to her. She slipped it into the toaster before she went to bed.

In the morning it was gone.

THANK YOU FOR READING THIS
FEIWEL AND FRIENDS BOOK.

The friends who made

Missy Piggle-Wiggle
and the
Sticky-Fingers Cure

possible are:

JEAN FEIWEL, Publisher

LIZ SZABLA, Associate Publisher

RICH DEAS, Senior Creative Director

HOLLY WEST, Editor

ALEXEI ESIKOFF, Senior Managing Editor

KIM WAYMER, Production Manager

ANNA ROBERTO, Editor

CHRISTINE BARCELLONA, Associate Editor

KAT BRZOZOWSKI, Editor

ANNA POON, Assistant Editor

EMILY SETTLE, Assistant Editor

CAROL LY, Designer

HAYLEY JOZWIAK, Managing Editor

Follow us on Facebook or visit us online at mackids.com.

Our books are friends for life.